D0951885

MIRACLE AT BELLEVUE

MIRACLE at BELLEVUE

Theodore Isaac Rubin, M.D.

MACMILLAN PUBLISHING COMPANY · NEW YORK

COLLIER MACMILLAN PUBLISHERS · LONDON

Macmillan Publishing Company
866 Third Avenue, New York, N.Y. 10022
Collier Macmillan Canada, Inc.

Library of Congress Cataloging-in-Publication Data

Rubin, Theodore Isaac.

Miracle at Bellevue.

I. Title.

PS3568.U293M5   1986   813'.54   86–16343

ISBN 0–02–605780–8

First Printing 1986

Designed by Jack Meserole

Printed in the United States of America

For TRUDY, *my daughter,*
with love.

ONE

There is no mediator between God's children and God.
—*Talmud J.:*
Berakoth, 9:1

Awakening

AND after two thousand years God woke up and he said:

"Usurpers and false prophets have bastardized my words and have lied and cheated for their own glory. Their greed and false messages have given comfort and power to the Evil One. And during my sleep the people of Earth through their diverse temples and religions worshiped him even as they spoke my name. And he gave them disease and pestilence and war. Maimed and suffering children abound. Cancer is rampant. Fake notions of morality and of the human condition sow confusion, self-hate, and insanity. Communication among people no longer exists. False churches preach that pleasure is sinful and that pain and self-denial are virtuous. Sanctimonious hypocrites are deified. Masochistic, grandiose monsters are worshiped. Rich and garish parasites rule—and my people, my own people, have been tortured, killed, decimated—all this in my name while I slept.

"You are my son, my only son. You are me on Earth. You were here, have suffered, have returned. Your given name, the name I gave you and give you now, is on their tongues. They knew him as Jesus, and you are the true Jesus now. I am not omnipotent. I shall need to sleep again. In the meantime changes must take place.

"Wake now Jesus. Lie to them Jesus. Guard your name and call yourself Harry until the moment of truth. Wake now. Secure your release. Enter the world. I love you."

Harry woke with a start. It was four in the morning. Everyone on the ward was still asleep.

 **T**WO

To love God truly, you must first love man. And if anyone tells you that he loves God but does not love his fellow man, he is lying.

—Hasidic saying

Jesus

"WHAT IS your name?" the head doctor asked.

My name is Jesus, he wanted to say. He bit his lip and tasted the salt of God's blood on his tongue and he lied and said,

"Harry. My name is Harry—Harry Byrd." And he knew he could do it. He would fool them.

"No more Jesus?" the young woman doctor smirked.

Harry answered a simple no.

"Do you want to leave the hospital?" asked the very old doctor.

"Yes."

"Can you take care of yourself, Harry?" the woman doctor asked, drawing out the sound of the name—H–a–r–r–y—as if it were a ridiculous notion they all really recognized.

"I don't know."

"Well, that's honest," one of them said and they all chimed in and seemed very pleased and Harry knew that God's love inspired him and he dared more.

"I can only try," he said, and now they seemed ecstatic.

He was discharged from the state mental institution somewhere in the Midwest and headed by bus to New York City.

7

Cleansing

FIVE-FIFTEEN P.M., a cloudy day. At Fifty-Seventh Street and Third Avenue, traffic is jammed in all directions. Horns blast. The icy cold air is thick with smog. Half a dozen people lean out of their cars, enraged. Some are cursing and red-faced. Two Third Avenue buses stuck at right angles to each other race their motors, rhythmically farting carbon-monoxide fumes into the smog. A uniformed chauffeur in a long gray limousine sits erect, formal, impassive. His passenger, an eleven- or twelve-year-old red-haired boy, lounges in back of the car flipping pages of a comic book—indifferent, seemingly unaware that they have not moved in fifteen minutes.

People on the street are elbowing, pushing, and shoving to see what is going on. A police-car siren screams inane, arrhythmic sounds. Several policemen elbow their way through an ever-increasing mass of people. One man yells to another,

"It's going-home-from-work showtime."

There she is in the middle of the intersection, tearing up shopping bags of miscellaneous odds and ends and throwing the contents at the gawkers. Shoes; an old clock; a fur coat—in good condition; packages of news-paper clippings tied together by shoelaces and ribbons; cans of sardines, salmon, and dog food; a can of shaving cream; tooth brushes—old and worn out; an old hair-dryer; several one-celled batteries; a man's cap; rolls of toilet paper; and more and more and still more small artifacts and symbols of twentieth-century America. She throws them all and then the bags themselves—more to rid herself of them than at the people and cars around her. Her face is red, streaked with dirt over ingrained grime. She shouts at the crowd and then looks up to the sky and implores God,

"Save us Jesus! Save us!" and then she is even more furious at the crowd. She picks up rolls of toilet paper and throws them and they streak out long ribbons and form a kind of decorative circle of which she is the hub. She then tears off her tattered clothes and throws these, too, screaming,

"Cleanse me Jesus!" and then begs and weeps in deep misery, tears streaking her cheeks.

She is obviously in great emotional pain. An old lady fairly close to her says,

"Do something for this woman, do something!"

A young woman says,

"Where the hell are the police?"

She is naked now. Her body is brick red. She is not as old as she looked dressed. Her breasts are high and full and cleanly white against the redness of the rest of her body. Her nipples are hard and purple with cold. Some boys snicker. Now she is on her knees. Her head is down. She moans and sways from side to side and whispers repeatedly,

"Jesus, cleanse me."

The police reach her, wrap her in a police-uniform jacket, and lead her to a waiting ambulance on the southeast corner of Fifty-Seventh and Third. She does not protest. She is silent. She clutches one possession to her breast—a small, oak-framed mirror. Two policemen gather her belongings as the ambulance pulls away. Two boys kick the empty shopping bags and rolls of toilet paper around for a few minutes. The crowd disappears instantly. Now the boys leave, too. The gutter is streaked with toilet paper.

Entrance Exam

"WHAT's your name?" the resident psychiatrist asked. She didn't answer. *Noncooperative*, he wrote.

"I'm a doctor and I want to help you." No comment by her. *Affect seems flat*, he wrote.

"My own name is Phillip Green," the young man said as gently as he knew how. "Everyone calls me Phil."

"Mary," she whispered.

"How did you get here, Mary?"

"Ambulance."

"I mean what brought you here—to the hospital?" He was pleased that his gentleness worked and he was so gentle now she barely heard him.

"Ambulance!" she screamed, giving him a considerable start. *Concrete thinking*, he wrote.

"What is your second name?" he asked, priding himself on his immediate recovery.

"Mary—first, second, third, fourth," she giggled, "and always." She seemed pleased.

Her gibberish and exaltation seem way out of line, he thought, and wrote his diagnosis:

Inappropriate affect and silliness possibly of hebephrenic origin.

"Do you think anything is wrong with you?" he asked.

"I'm clean now," she said quietly. After a moment she added, "And I'm ready."

Thought disorder, he wrote.

"Ready for what?" he asked, ever so gently.

"For what?" she screamed. She stood up, glared at him, and then paced up and back the small admitting room. "For what?" she raged.

He was frightened and thought of calling in an attendant or perhaps giving her a shot of Thorazine. But his pride held him down and in a shaky hand he wrote,

Inappropriate behavior.

She came up close to him and screamed in his face— nose-to-nose now—and he was terrified.

"For what? . . . you dare call him a 'what'? Go into the cold. Strip yourself of everything and return purified."

"I'm sorry, I'm sorry," he blurted as quickly as he could. "Please sit down. For whom?" He patted the chair.

"For *him!*" she blasted in his ear. "For *him!* Do you understand?"

"Yes," he said and she sat down and volunteered,

"That's why I'm here. I came here to wait for *him.* I'm Mary, do you understand? I'm Mary."

"Mary who?" he dared again, admiring his own courage and professionalism.

"Mary, Mother of God," she said in a coarse, strident voice.

"Mary Magdalene," she said in an oily, sexy seductive voice.

"All the Marys in the world," she said matter-of-factly.

Delusional, he wrote.

She smiled at him benevolently.

"I didn't mean to frighten you, my son." She spoke calmly now, in a serene voice. Her manner was sweet and gentle and in no way patronizing. The scene had become one between a caring mother and a needy adult son.

"I am the Holy Mother and in this way I really am all the mothers in the world, the mother of all sons—yourself as well. But mainly I am *his* mother and I've been sent here to wait for *his* arrival."

Delusions of grandeur, he wrote, *with much of the usual religious overtones*, but he thought the words *religious crap.*

"This is no crap," she stated, the mothering tone gone now and replaced by an imperious authority.

"Never said it was," he replied respectfully and wrote, *paranoid schizophrenic* and thought, *crazier than hell* and then had the further thought as he rang for the nurse—*screw you lady!*

As the nurse led her from the room her last words to him were,

"I'm as pure as driven snow now Doctor and I've come here by ambulance and I'm here in order to wait for Jesus. And I'll know when I see him because I'm Mary." Her affect this time was in keeping with her words. Then she turned and said,

"Don't think harshly of me Doctor. Jesus loves you and Mary does, too."

Mary

"I've been assigned to your case."

"Case?"

"To you," he quickly added. "I'm your doctor. My name is Kline, Dr. Kline." He held out his hand. She ignored it.

"How do you feel?" he asked.

"I'm as old as the world," she sighed.

"You think I'm too young to help you?"

She ignored him.

"Can you tell me how you feel? Did you sleep alright? Is there anything I can do for you? Do you need a sleeping pill at night? Are you eating alright? They told me you've lost five pounds since you've been here. Do you know how long you've been here?"

"You're full of questions, David," she answered gently.

After a few minutes of silence she answered his questions.

"I've been here just short of a week. My orientation is fairly good. My weight is excellent. I feel empty."

"Can you tell me about feeling empty?"

"It's exactly how I want to feel—empty and clean—more than clean, immaculate. I am empty and receptive—ready to receive him."

"How long have you been on the street?"

"A long time."

"We realized who you are a few days ago."

"You're a good boy, David."

"Boy? I'm almost thirty-five."

"I'm as old as time itself—so you see, I'm not patronizing you."

"Some of the staff remembered seeing you in plays on Broadway. They say you were very good."

"I've walked in the desert. You call it the street. And I'm very good—now."

"Do you think you would like to leave here soon? Is there anyone you would like us to contact? You seem to have given up the Mary—" He hesitated and she filled in for him,

"Role."

"Yes."

Now she was formal, full of dignity, and pronounced each word with meticulous care.

"This is no role, Dr. Kline. Whomever you and your staff have mistaken me for no longer exists. I am Mary! I am empty. I am receptive. I will receive him when he arrives and this is the place. There is no one for you to contact. We will contact you, in time."

She left the small office and headed back to the large day room.

On the chart he noted that her orientation was good and that there was no overt evidence of organic brain damage. He added that he could perceive a strong hysterical flavor not uncommon in former actresses. It was too early to tell whether her delusion was fixed and of deep schizophrenic roots or a transient hysterical phase. He recommended retaining the admitting diagnosis of *schizophrenic reaction, paranoid type* for the time being and a prolonged period of observation.

He was interested in her case.

This was his first real celebrity—former celebrity.

Father and Son

I have to get back the feel of myself. This phrase repeated itself to him again and again. But he could not feel himself. When he reached in and tried, he felt an inner hollowness and this terrified him. He pictured sounds bouncing off empty walls—dull thuds—and wondered if the inner core of himself had not somehow died and disintegrated.

The room was small. A bed, a dresser, a hard chair, a small round table, and an old art-deco torch lamp filled it almost completely. He kept the lamp lit nearly all the time but it had little effect on the darkness he felt inside.

Again and again he tried with words to describe how he felt, but it didn't work. He almost believed that if he could verbalize the feeling, really verbalize it perfectly, that somehow then the central problem of himself would be solved and all would finally be well.

Jagged, he told himself—he felt jagged, like a jagged end of something—anything—and he pictured a piece of wood somehow splintered off of a large smooth board. Then, in his mind's eye, he saw a wide, deep stream of water with many small tributary branches feeding into the main body at all kinds of irregular—crazy—angles. Suddenly, the main stream was gone. Only the branches remained. Their contents went this way and that, spilling out in sprays and drips and small pressured torrents, having no main pool to collect them.

He shivered uncontrollably. The word *wasted* came to his mind and hung in the emptiness of himself like a black neon sign. The shivering stopped. That was it, he thought. He had lost the main stream. He had become all those fragmented tributaries. Could it be connected? The sign, *wasted*, was no longer lit. Could he get back the feel of himself? Had he ever had it? Was there ever a main stream? Had he ever felt differently?

He wasn't sure anymore. He had tried to keep the past down and out. Review upon review of everything since birth—some of it called "treatment"—had taken place again and again and it only hurt and made him feel more scattered. He thought of it all as *back there* and he tried to keep it all back there but he couldn't always do it. Fragments and torrents—isolated words, pictures, smells, sounds, and feelings—often intruded themselves despite his willing them dead and buried. The isolated bits and pieces seldom made sense. But he had an advantage over them because they were usually there and gone, too fleeting to affect his conscious NOW of things most of the time.

There were other times, however, when whole strings of scenes, feelings, and sentences would come through and inundate him so completely that it took the strongest conscious effort not to lose touch with the present. There had been a few horrible times when he had been drowned in this kind of emotional, chaotic maelstrom for hours. His emergence back to present consciousness and the reestablishment of self-control seemed to have nothing to do with effort on his part or anyone else's. He knew that the maelstrom was born of the past but he repudiated the past for a more powerful reason. This horror-producing past was only a fragment of his being. It wasn't even a fragment—only an artifact.

There was a past beyond that past which encompassed all time and stretched in all directions, to infinity and beyond. The ruler of that *Forever Time* was his parent—his only parent and recognition by him as his Son would end the struggle and bring permanent peace.

Cover-up

HE WOKE at four in the morning and thought, *I've got no cover-up.* He tried to chuck the thought and slip back into sleep. Maybe he could convert it into a dream. Sometimes he was able to weave a dream and more sleep around a prickly thought that nudged him awake. But this one was too strong. He could not generate effective diluting embroidery. Even as a little sleep came back, it was there—big, heavy, and getting heavier. It refused to go away.

He woke more fully, not quite completely, just enough to think of other things. But now it was in command. Other things were pushed aside and then there were no other things. The intruder had taken over. *No cover-up!* He would have to think it out of existence or it would plague him for hours, even longer. After several minutes—with sleep for now gone—it made sense. As Harry he was bits and pieces, fragments of raw sensations, without an interstitial connecting fabric and without a cover-up. In the hospital he had met a number of people who lacked inner connection. But it seemed to him that they had some kind of cover-up. Their bleeding points did not show. No blood leaked through to the surface. He thought of Christ on the cross and looked at his palms. There was nothing unusual about them. Then he got up and looked in the mirror. His face showed it—the agony he felt—the terrible vulnerability—the open sensitivity to anything, to every-thing—no protective armor at all—no cover-up. He thought of his face as his bleeding point, as the surface which was no surface at all. And yet his face fooled people, other people, not himself. Because it was the sensitive, pale, thirty-year-old face of a blue-eyed man named Harry, desperately trying to hold on to that picture—a man named—Harry. But *Harry* provided no cover-up, no connections, only agonized fragments and blood leaking out and wasting—though it didn't show in the mirror.

Alone

WALKING in the city very early in the morning he felt that he was an empty world in an empty world, inter-rupted by disconnected flash-fragments of words and occasional feelings. But the feelings usually coagulated into painful anxiety and so he welcomed the emptiness even as he envied the rare passerby who seemed to him inordinately full of life.

He had not walked far from his room, and when the streets started filling up with people, he headed back and thought about resurrection. Perhaps this was death, and rebirth was possible. He thought of the dream, of God and of Jesus, and a sense of combined sweetness and wholeness flooded him. But as he entered his room the sensation vanished. He was Harry after all—empty and yet full of anxiety.

Exploration and Preparation

"You simply can't wander all over the place." He said it as kindly as he could.

"But I'm on an open ward," she said patiently, as if they had been through this before, which they hadn't.

"Yes, but people can't wander all over the building." He matched her patience with his own.

"You mean we patients can't, Dr. Kline. Doctors and staff people can. Those of us who are privileged enough to be on a so-called *open ward* are really supposed to be well enough to understand this bit of duplicity."

All this said by her in the same kindly voice, now more closely an imitation of his voice and manner. She was an exceptional mimic. He picked up the impersonation but ignored it completely, retaining his composure, and carefully and kindly asked,

"Duplicity?"

"We are supposed to be well enough to be on an open ward, which means that we are clear enough in mind to know that open means as closed as a closed ward even though the door isn't locked. The door is open, Dr. Kline—but only for you, not for us. For us it is closed even though it is open."

Now she had his voice down perfectly. It was as if he heard himself talking to himself. He laughed good-naturedly and said something about the considerable talent she had for mimicry. But now she countered in her own voice and manner that he was alluding to her talent rather than the issue. He evaded the issue and asked,

"Why do you wander around so much anyway? Is it restlessness, curiosity?"

"It's for him!" she answered. "I'm preparing his parish. I want to be able to introduce him to everyone who needs his help."

"Do you know when or how he will arrive? Do you get messages from him?" He felt relieved that he had been able to get her off the open/closed ward issue and into some of the substance of her pathology. But he was an honest man and he felt guilty, too, using her sickness to get himself off the hook of her logic.

"I hear no voices. I receive no messages. No hallucinations in this particular nut, Dr. Kline. He will arrive. He's done it before. He'll do it again."

"Before?"

"A few thousand years ago. Dr. Kline, I suppose people are just as duplicitous now as they were then and need him just as badly. I know what you are thinking."

"What?"

"Pure case of paranoid schizophrenia. Delusions of grandeur."

"You're wrong. I was thinking why would he come here, first stop?"

"Because this is the most famous lunatic asylum in the world, Dr. Kline. And because among these lunatics he will find his disciples and will realize and experience his own growth. And among them he will learn how to help the really sick ones outside—the ones who are supposed to be sane—the ones beyond open and closed wards, Dr. Kline—the ones who are always locked up in layers and layers of duplicity."

He sighed and said he would see her the next day. She left his office and continued to explore the building.

Tunnels

THREE DAYS LATER she discovered the tunnels.

They reminded her of the tunnels under the city streets she had slept in when the weather got too cold for doorways. But these had no steam. They were cold and empty. She immediately took to calling them *catacombs*, which gave her a good religious feeling and further confirmed the righteousness of her mission. They hadn't been used in years, indeed there was hardly anybody left who knew they existed. They stretched in all directions fairly deep under all the buildings and it took her very little time to realize that they made any spot in the hospital accessible with ease. In three more days she knew the maze by heart and could pop up just about anywhere almost at will.

She had always prided herself on her sense of direction and her years of living on the streets had sharpened this gift to a fine edge. Interestingly, nobody even noticed her as she wandered in and out of halls, wards, and rooms and disappeared again back to her open ward in the psychiatric division of the hospital.

In another week she had been almost all over, even in several operating theaters and intensive-care units. She had not been an actress for nothing, and acting like a visitor and sometimes an ambulatory patient made her virtually invisible among the crowded halls and rooms. Several times she felt noticed and took on a role of authority and no one interfered with her. By the second week of her arrival she knew every spot of the entire complex better than anyone alive or for that matter better than anyone ever had.

It took her only minutes to get to the pediatric wards, obstetrical section, surgical floors, and to places where people lay moaning and dying. She never went outside. She did it all through the catacombs and she felt increasingly prepared for his arrival.

Psychiatric Consultation

AT THE STAFF CONFERENCE Kline reviewed her case and conceded that she was far from the usual "bag lady."

Dr. Stephen Morton, chief of the section and a man in his late fifties, said that there didn't seem to be a common syndrome among bag ladies.

Dr. Jackson Miller, the chief clinical psychologist, said that most of the street people—bag ladies and bag men, too—were deteriorated schizophrenics.

Dr. Kline said there was little that was deteriorated about Betty Smith. He went on to say that she ignored him when he referred to her by her real name, which had also been her stage name.

Someone laughed and said that her current stage name was Mary.

Morton asked which Mary she was.

"All the Marys in the world," Phillip Green, the young resident, answered. He went on to give her admitting-room explanation.

Kline added that she was extremely well oriented and hyper-logical, which he realized was quite common in paranoids, and seemed to harbor an encapsulated delusion.

Morton agreed, recalling to them the woman he had treated for years who was perfectly OK as long as you didn't mention the FBI. If you did, it kicked off a long psychotic tirade which disappeared the moment the subject was changed.

Someone asked if her blood work-up had been done to make sure there was no syphilis.

The chief nurse said of course, and that the V.D.R.O. test was negative. She wondered if this question wasn't a prejudice, one against actresses. She had once aspired to a career on the stage.

Dr. Kline stated that there was no evidence at all of organic brain damage and that her physical health seemed to be excellent.

Dr. Morton said that this too seemed to be commonplace in people who lived on the street but who were not alcoholics.

Not always, Dr. Alan Smith, a medical resident, stated, pointing out cases of pneumonia and TB they had picked up on the medical wards.

Dr. Morton graciously conceded, "I stand corrected." But then he added dryly, "I don't really believe in encapsulated delusions. I think if you probe enough you eventually realize that the capsule includes the entire personality. They may latch on to a particular facet but paranoia is like cancer. If it's there on a psychotic level it metastasizes through the entire personality. How about some Thorazine?"

"And then back on the streets," Jackson Miller muttered.

"The city doesn't pay us to keep them here," Dr. Morton replied mildly.

"She'll never take it," Kline said.

"How do you know?" Smith asked.

"She's convinced nothing is wrong with her."

"Nothing new about that," the internist replied. "Besides, why tell her it's Thorazine?"

"New rules are we tell everyone everything," Sara Kalinsky, the social worker, stated. "And besides, we like it that way," she added with an obvious effort at courage.

"Thorazine would put her on the street in a fog," the chief nurse added.

"That's been our job for the last five years," Morton reminded her and then added, "Let's keep her as is for the moment. After all, she's our only current celebrity. Next case."

Alice Remsen, the chief nurse, put another folder on his desk.

The Anxiety Attack

HE JUST WALKED into a store as *a Harry Byrd* and shopped—this time no thinking, no consciousness of himself, no preplanning. The things were there in his room to remind him—cans of tuna and salmon, flat tins of sardines, bread and butter. But he thought about this too long and it brought back awareness of himself—*a stranger-standing-off-looking-at-a-foreign-body kind of feeling*—and he was under siege. The anxiety attack was like a reprimand for taking too much time off from himself. His heart raced so fast he could not breathe.

He felt like he was being engulfed by a big black hole. He hyperventilated and nearly passed out and then he screamed his anguish, screamed it out,

"Oh help me God, help me, help me!" and tears streamed down his face and he cried convulsively. This kind of sobbing had never happened before and it ended the anxiety attack. The shaking stopped. His heart slowed. Terrible awareness of himself—the separation feeling—disappeared—the black hole around him was gone. He lay back on the bed exhausted.

When he woke up, he looked at the groceries and awareness of himself began to return. He jumped up from the bed and rushed into the street.

Purification

ANXIETY ATTACKS had become addictive. They terrified him and the pain of terror was excruciating. And yet there was an irresistible temptation to bring them on and he did and regretted it each time that he did. Self-awareness did it. It got to a point where he brought them on just thinking about himself.

The street was the antidote. The stimulation of the street activity took him away from himself, diluted awareness and cut the attacks. Wandering about the street he dared to think about it. He concluded that it was the control and the pain. This was the one thing he could bring on—anxiety attacks—and in a perverse way this gave him self-mastery—over something. And the pain killed emptiness. It was a feeling, a very alive feeling, albeit a deadly one.

In no time at all he became so expert that he could bring on a self-imposed panic at will. Then it got to the point where he couldn't will it otherwise. It was as if a stronger will forced him to will the attacks upon himself. He fled into the street a hundred times a day— the small room had come to represent the place for generation of his new affliction. Perhaps going to a hospital would be the best thing. He thought of Bellevue. They would put him on medication. The attacks would cease. But then he would surely be what a fellow patient had called "one of the walking dead." Besides, he knew this wouldn't last. His real life was going to begin soon. This was a kind of hellfire he had to go through. Without verbalizing all of this, he felt that a kind of terrible purifying process was going on and that he could only undergo it as combined human fragments known as Harry.

In the street he found relief but he had to go back to the room to eat and to sleep. Harry, nonhospitalized Harry, was of this earth after all.

Walks

As TIME PASSED the attacks became less frequent. He thought that perhaps the mechanism which generated them had become worn down. Or maybe it was because he spent most of his time in the street.

Without thought or decision he developed the habit of taking very long walks. They were of two kinds. One consisted of exhausting, rapid-paced, forced marches of great distance—in which his eyes remained fixed forward and an unbroken, steady, military rhythm was immediately established. This kind of walk permitted little observation but provided much exercise. Distance was covered—big for the city—sometimes ten miles or more a day. He thought of these as anxiety dissipators. He had always been quite thin but the walks made his body hard and seemed to reduce his appetite so that he had to spend less time in his room eating.

The other kind of walks were shorter. They were fast, slow, smooth, jerky, and went in all directions, never straight lines, sometimes covering the same areas several times a day. He wasn't aware of it but they took place when he was less anxious and usually after the forced-march type had taken place. In these walks he saw, heard, smelled, and felt the city sights, noises, smells, and feelings. With the forced walk it was as if each day had a new distant, unseen goal which drew him without diversion or interruption in a straight line to completion. In the second, he went this way and that, attracted here by a sound, there by a sight, back again by a feeling, around the corner by a possibility. With both walks he crisscrossed the city and unwittingly came to know it. He passed Bellevue many times and without conscious awareness its presence loomed large in the schema of the city he came to form in his mind.

The City

HIS FEELINGS about the city developed into two principle forms.

In one, the city was a kind of electric force field— the center of which had great power in the form of massive buildings, important offices, and the dwellings of obviously prestigious, powerful, and rich people. The entertainment areas were breaks in the field, kinds of safety valves through which excess force and energy were dissipated into the atmosphere. Quiet, elegant streets off main centers contained reserves of power. And there were peripheral places—the poor neighborhoods, with no connection to any power source—scarcely alive and only so because of some proximity to overflowing strength from power areas. His own room was on the very edge of a power reserve area, barely connected by a string of respectable but not elegant brown-stones. His building, in fact, was the very beginning of the depleted area which rapidly degenerated so that five streets away power was virtually dead. For about a mile in this direction people of all colors and nation-alities lived in a slum of crowded, small apartments in dark, narrow, dirty streets, seemingly oblivious to the cultural advantages of living in the greatest city in the world. Yet this area attracted him. The electric force concept persisted and in this construct, this was the deadest area of all. But there was another schema, and when it was applied, this dead area—this power vac-uum area—was the most alive area of all.

This was the *People Schema* and it, too, was with him constantly. In this plan, the center of the city was the place where real people lived: children; old and young adults; beautiful and ugly people; healthy, sick and crippled people; people with all kinds of mongrel dogs; people who made all kinds of common people noises— who made no effort to mute their feelings with super-imposed ideas of gentility, so that they laughed, wept, screamed out loud; people who sometimes drank too much and cursed and fought in many accents and in a variety of foreign-based idioms; people who threw garbage, particularly empty beer cans, into the street, and who generally seemed oblivious to middle- and upper-class niceties; people who played stickball and sweated in hot weather and played with running noses and frozen ears and fingertips in cold weather—but who had not been air-conditioned out of knowing the different feelings changes in the weather brought. This was the center—the *People Center*. He had once heard the word *funky* and it was right for this area. This was the *Alive People Funky Center*. It brought to mind connotations of dark, warm, strong, germinating life forces.

The entertainment area was a simulated facsimile of this *Alive People Center*. He saw it as used to stimulate people from *Dead People Centers* into feeling for a moment and believing that they were alive, too. But the aliveness generated by the entertainment area was mechanical, short-lived, and like all imitations only superficial at best. It could not mitigate vast storehouses of accumulated emotional deadness. It could not dilute the effects of living on elegant, dead streets, in elegant, dead apartment houses with dead, uniformed doormen walking elegant, dead, uniformly clipped mechanical poodles and working in huge mausoleum buildings—cold, corporate, indifferent buildings which seemed to guard a cemetery of dead feelings like monolithic gravestones of an era not yet here and already gone.

This was the *Center of Deadness*. Here, he saw many cardboard figures. From a distance they looked alive, like real people, but when he got up close he could tell. What gave them away was that he could see that they were acting—all doing some kind of learned, right thing—walking the right way, saying right things, making right expressions with their eyes and eyebrows—right—all of it right and appropriate but all of it learned and memorized—none of it spontaneous, free-flowing and natural—all of it pretty interesting for a little while and then boring because none of it was hooked to any real passion. Here and there someone looked real and it seemed that a real live thing would come through but a closer look always revealed the cardboard look and fidelity to the status of the walking dead. Sometimes actual movement and real features would break through in children, seemingly destroying the shellac their parents had provided. But the freeze-up and proper behavior would be quickly reinstated and spontaneity put down as feelings were deadened.

He enjoyed the *Center of Deadness*. By contrast it made him feel alive. But then a yearning for contact—only sight contact but contact nevertheless—with real people would fill him. This was in no way a craving for larger involvement, which was completely out of his scope at this time. But contact, however fleeting and superficial, motivated him powerfully. This would hit him, fill him, and send him almost running to the *Alive People Center* where people of no consequence lived in a power vacuum.

And then snow and freezing weather came and he had to stay in his room.

The Surgeon-Patient

THE MORPHINE worked. He was in a comfortable, half-sleep haze and then he saw her coming toward him.

"Can I help you?" she asked.

"No," he replied.

"I've been here before and you were asleep."

"Are you a nurse?" He was thick-tongued but he didn't care.

"No."

"A volunteer?" He felt very sleepy, kind of dreamy. *Hypnagogic reverie*, he thought.

"I'm a patient," she said, "and my name is Mary."

"I'm a patient," he said, "and I'm dying. The hangman also dies, you know."

"Hangman?"

"I'm a surgeon." The morphine had really hit and he felt very foggy. "I'm dying." He hesitated, not knowing how to put it and then added, "I'm dying in my own specialty."

"Your own specialty?"

"Of a disease I used to make a living from." He was almost asleep but this bit of cynicism pleased him so much it woke him a little. "Colon," he said groggily. "Carcinoma—that's cancer—of the splenic flexure with metastases to the spleen and liver. I'm through. An open-and-shut case."

She just listened.

"How many I've opened and shut through the years without doing a thing. Look at me. Can you believe I was once a big strong man?" He was fully awake now but still anxiety- and pain-free from the morphine. "Once was—once was was only seven months ago. I obstructed seven months ago. I knew what it was right away. I called it right. Jesus, if I wouldn't, who would?

My life started to drain away seven months ago. Can you imagine I'm on chemicals, radiation, cobalt—the whole blast. Foolishness! It's hopeless. How many times I've had identical cases. Didn't know what to tell them. Now . . . the hangman also dies finally." He suddenly marveled at how much talking he was doing—much more than at any other time since the disaster began.

"You were never a hangman," she said.

"There were so many I never helped," he replied.

"You couldn't or you would have."

"That's true. Oh God I would have."

"Is there anything I can do for you, anything at all? Maybe if I can do something for somebody, he will come. I thought I knew we would meet here. But now I'm beginning to have serious doubts and I'm thinking of leaving."

"He? Who is he? Who are you waiting for?" But he lost interest in the questions. The morphine and his condition combined suddenly to make him feel muddled and removed.

She went very close to him and then she kissed him on the forehead and held his hand in her two hands.

"Tell me what I can do for you," she implored. "I want, I need, to do something for you. Not just for him to come. Not just that but for you—just for you."

He was awake now, alert again.

"I want to cry," he said. "More than anything, I want to cry."

She sat down on his bed and put his head on her bosom and kissed his forehead. From up close she saw how wasted he was. His eyes were sunken and his limbs were very thin. His belly was bloated. She re-membered hospitals and patients she had visited as an actress.

"Cry," she said, "cry." And she held his hand and stroked his head and cheek and he cried and cried and then surrendered all control and sobbed for a full ten minutes before his crying subsided.

"Thank you," he said. "Thank you. You've been better for me than any treatment I've received to date."

The morphine had worn off but he fell into a very deep sleep which obliterated all pain.

Patients Talking

SHE FELT BETTER TOO and returned to the surgeon-pa-tient's room two and even three times a day. They spoke and found out some of the essentials about each other.

His name was Henry Salter. He was fifty-six years old and widowed. He had a married daughter and two grandsons who lived in Dallas. His son-in-law was a surgeon, and he withstood his family's pleas to come to a hospital in Texas. He wanted to be home and Bellevue was almost home since he had trained, worked, and taught there most of his life, and he did not want to burden them. They had visited him frequently during the seven months and his daughter Madelene had remained in New York for three weeks (before Mary met him) to be at his side. She had returned to Texas at his insistence a week earlier. He did not want her to see him again. He knew he would be moribund before very long and he did not want her or her husband Mike to remember him that way. He was surprised at how much he missed them and especially his grandsons, since he had been rather detached since his wife Carol's death. But there was nothing else to be done about it now.

He never told Mary how Carol died, only that she had been gone for more than ten years and that he had filled the awful vacuum her death brought by burying himself in work. He told Mary that he thought about this as a possible causative factor in his illness. "Perhaps lack of emotional involvement paralyzed the autoimmunological system, making susceptibility to malignancy possible." He didn't really know. He told her he was not at all religious but that he was a Jew.

She liked him very much and saw him as a person of openness, warmth, and charm. Even in his wasted, extraordinarily painful condition she liked the look and feel of him. His being a Jew drew her to him even more. She liked Jews. Jesus was a Jew.

He was not shocked in the least at what she told him about herself. Indeed, the only thing that seemed strange at all was his total acceptance of her and her state of being. He attributed this to his condition. His perception of the world and priorities had changed radically.

"I was an actress. I thought I loved it. I became a

nonentity. As I became more and more successful I shrunk. I felt myself disappearing inside. I became nothing. Then I started coming late. Then I missed dates. People in the business hated me. I hated me. And eventually I faded out and disappeared. I became nobody." She stopped to think for a while and he fell asleep for a few minutes and then woke when she spoke again.

"I became a street person. I don't remember how I got there. One day I woke in a doorway. I had become a street person. In very cold weather I slept under-ground—next to New York heat pipes. I had lost my-self. I was nobody. I was nothing. Then it happened. He spoke to me. At night while I slept I heard him."

"You dreamed," he suggested.

"No! It was no dream. Just his voice to me. And he called me Mary and I became someone again. He said it didn't matter where I'd go. Just let it happen and his son would come to me. His son and mine. And then he told me and I stripped myself of all worldly goods and I became purified and I let myself go with the tide—his tide, you see—and I was washed ashore here. And here is where I knew he would come. But now I'm not sure. I have not heard his voice again. Shall I wait?"

"Wait," he said reassuringly. He didn't know why but he felt it was the right thing to say and in his morphine haze he said it again. "Wait, wait."

She left feeling more at peace. Somehow through this dying man who was very close to him, he had told her and she would wait.

Steiner

GREGORY STEINER waited too. He went to conferences. He made rounds and grand rounds. He went to lectures. He read. But he waited for the patient who would really interest him, the patient who could teach him and whom he could help. He was offered a number of candidates for treatment, but none was right. He was not only a resident in psychiatry. He was also a student at the Analytic Institute and he wanted a patient with whom he could use psychoanalytic dynamics and principles to maximum advantage. He waited.

He had his wife. They were young. But they had been together for so long now and they were so close. He could wait for anything and anyone as long as he had her.

Alone

IT SNOWED continuously for four days. For years people would talk of the great snowstorm of that late winter. The storm was accompanied by very low temperatures and stinging winds. The streets of the city were almost deserted. He couldn't stand the cold, and imprisonment in his room brought back the attacks of anxiety with a vengeance. The snow made it worse. It contributed to a sense of deep silence—a cold, white, muffling deadness.

His utter aloneness brought on terrible self-consciousness again and again, and with this, panic became intensified. He ran outside and into the snow several times. But coldness and the snow-silence made things worse. There were no people even in the middle of the *Alive People Center*. At one point he ran to Bellevue and he saw lights and people through lower-floor windows. It was inviting and this urge to go on in frightened him and he ran back to his room, cold, wet, and in a terrible state of anxiety. He felt a massive weight in his chest. He wanted to scream out more than anything, to cry, to sob, to rid himself of the crushing feeling. But the scream wouldn't come. Then he beat the wall with his fists—harder and harder until his knuckles bled—but there was little pain and no weeping at all. But this exhausted him and he lay down on the bed fully clothed and surprisingly fell into a deep sleep in several minutes, despite his anxiety.

The Cauldron

AND IN THAT SLEEP it happened.

He was back in the West. There was a shepherd in the sky. He was herding the clouds into a vast reserve area. They would be used for rain wherever they were needed. They would bring life to dry desert areas.

And then his true father spoke to him.

"You have walked through the desert.

"Be who you are.

"Go into the cauldron. Help those who will be helped.

"Bring them the comfort of human reality.

"You are my blood, you are whole now."

He woke.

He felt whole—anxiety-free.

A quantum change had taken place. He had his father's wisdom.

And he knew that Bellevue was the cauldron. It was still snowing but it didn't bother him at all. He headed there at once.

Betty Smith

"MORE AND MORE I think of myself as Betty Smith, and it feels awful. The good feel—the glow—disappears. I feel withered inside and pushed back to the street and to being no one. But I know he will come. I know who I am."

He said very gently, "Is it so important to be Mary? I mean could you feel who you are, really are, as either Betty or Mary?"

"No," she said with a resigned sigh. "I am really myself as Mary. And most important, as Mary I am connected to him. Do you think he is already here and just hasn't made himself known to me yet? Or perhaps he's on his way?"

"Perhaps," he said. He marveled at how he, Henry Salter, had become some kind of a psychotherapist. Indeed they were cotherapists of a sort—each comforting the other. He wondered which of them was crazier. But he was also aware that his periods of tolerable pain had become noticeably longer. But Salter had not been a surgeon for twenty-five years for nothing. He knew that his days were numbered.

THREE

God could not be everywhere, so he created mothers.

—Jewish saying

He who truly loves another can read his thoughts.

—*The Korester Rabbi*

The Message

HER DOUBTS reached a pinnacle on the evening he arrived. Later on she would think of her awful feelings of that night as the message, as the signal that he had come.

Despite her struggle, the feeling of being Betty Smith pervaded her more and more that day. With it came the certain knowledge that if it continued she would soon be back on the street and sleeping under the pipes.

She could get no comfort from Henry Salter. He was also going through a particularly bad period and required very heavy doses of morphine, which kept him in a deep stupor. Despite efforts to the contrary, she spent that day wolfing down food as she had sometimes done on the streets.

She could hardly resist the urge to accumulate all kinds of disconnected rubbish as her feeling of inner emptiness grew.

Entrance Exam

"YOUR ADMISSION note says that you believe you are the Son of God."

"No, Dr. Steiner. Not the Son of God. God's son."

"What's the difference?"

"Aren't we all God's sons and daughters, Dr. Steiner?"

"Then you feel that you are not singled out and special?"

"Each of us is special."

"You know what this place is?"

"Of course I know."

"What is it?"

"Are you testing my orientation?"

"Yes, I guess I am."

"This is not a therapeutic dialogue then?"

"How is that?"

"I was told that I was to be interviewed by you as a possible candidate for treatment, psychotherapy, by you, I presume."

"That's true."

"But your question is to elicit information about my mental status. It's in the form of a test. Forgive me if I sound pedantic or patronizing or—" He hesitated. ". . . all this intellectualizing. But this kind of questioning is anti-therapeutic, anti-free-associative and is characteristic of a clinical evaluation rather than a therapeutic encounter."

46

Steiner smiled. He was hooked. This was not the patient he was waiting for. He knew this man was crazy, really crazy, too crazy for supervision in the Institute, but he was hooked. This man had what an Institute teacher had once called "psychiatric charisma."

The People

HE HAD no interest in the hospital as a physical structure. His total concentration was on the people; so much so that he was oblivious to the inner geography of the place and had to be led about almost like a blind man by anyone of whom he asked directions.

The patients were a heterogeneous group and he decided that their most common characteristic was poverty. A well-to-do patient was a rarity in a city or state psychiatric institution.

The patients ranged from the severely disturbed and completely out-of-contact to those who seemed as well-composed as anyone on the street. There was no apparent effort to separate men and women except in the sleeping rooms. He felt an affinity and understanding for all of them and was filled with a sense of warm, comfortable benevolence in their presence. He had arrived. Among them he was at home.

He wandered through the open wards and early on realized how quiet it was. His memory of his own hospitalization was different. He did not consider this a hospitalization for himself. He was on a mission and he knew that the first person who needed his help was Steiner.

Contact

HE ASKED HER how to get to the large day room.

"You've finally come," she said. "I've waited. I knew. You need ask nobody else for directions again."

A feeling of infinite peace pervaded her. She now had a self. His self was her self. They were one and she felt strong.

As for him—he knew, as soon as she had spoken, that they were linked, that they were both part of a unity, children of his Father's wisdom. And he felt very strong.

Roma Berlino

PERHAPS the day room was a microcosm of the world. Every kind of language was spoken, including secret ones composed of neologisms which only the composer could understand. And there were people whose absolute silence spoke of their distrust, hopelessness, and isolation. And there were lucid ones—whose lucidity and logic had burned out all other evidence of humanity including feelings of any kind.

There was one man whose communication consisted of only two words, "Roma Berlino," which he shouted as if through a bullhorn every twelve minutes.

And there was a man who got up on a table and made speeches in an unknown tongue after each meal. Few listened and nobody understood. And, as with all other human worlds, there were microcosms within microcosms and seclusive and private worlds within worlds. And there were people within people in whom conversations took place among several autonomous personalities, some arguing for possession of a single body. And there were people paralyzed and stiffened by rage and others who moved in slow motion, their muscles bound by depression. There were others who could not sit still, who moved jerkily and constantly. Some were agitated and argued constantly with unseen inner visions and voices. A few searched for tears from sources long since dried up and a few wept constantly

without tears. And there were those who dressed me-
ticulously, conforming and compliant to the style of the
day, and others who tore their clothes off, and others
in bathrobes and gray hospital uniforms, and others
who were oblivious to sex, and others who were ob-
sessed with it, and of course the fat and thin and ugly
and beautiful ones. And to him and to her they were
all beautiful.

But he knew that they were struggling—all of them—
to be heard, to be recognized, to be understood, to be
dignified in some way—to be.

There was something else they had in common. He
knew by comparing them to day room populations he
had known when he was a patient. The expression of
themselves was muted. While they each spoke their
own language, it was not with the intensity and free
expressions they could have felt. He knew it. He knew
they were zonked out of it by drugs, Thorazine mostly,
he suspected.

Then he walked over to Roma Berlino thinking, *My
father sent me here for a rehearsal. This is all a rehearsal for
a larger stage.*

Mary and he walked over—very close—to the man
who shouted Roma Berlino at them in a muffled, very
hoarse voice. And Jesus said,

"Roma Berlino," and the man stood riveted and
then Jesus and Mary sang out,

"Roma Berlino," with as much force as they could
muster. Now the man answered them with rapid, mul-
tiple Roma Berlinos, ignoring the periodicity he prac-
ticed before. Then a few more patients, one who had
been mute for weeks, also shouted,

"Berlino, Berlino," and then Jesus reached out and took the man's hand, and Mary's, and she took the mute patient's hand, and soon there were six of them in the middle of the day room, joyously and with complete abandon shouting,

"Roma Berlino!"

And then the six of them laughed and laughed and tears streamed down the cheeks of Roma, as Jesus now thought of him, and the former mute man who carefully whispered to Mary,

"You know my name is Frank."

Therapy

"WAS the man called Jesus two thousand years ago psychotic, Dr. Steiner?"

"That's an interesting opening remark," Steiner answered gently.

"But not a free-association?" he smiled.

That's exactly what Steiner had thought—*Not a free-association*. He also thought that the purpose of the remark was to immediately put him on the defensive as a very effective form of resistance. He sought to counter this.

"But what shall I call you—what name?" Steiner asked.

"Whatever you like," he answered mildly, shrugging his shoulders.

"You called yourself Jesus when you first came here." Steiner smiled.

"Every place has its entry ticket." He smiled back.

"You mean you said you were Jesus in order to get in?" Very, very gently now, he thought.

"You wanted to know what to call me?" He seemed a bit irritated.

"Yes."

"Does calling me Jesus put it all into focus?"

"You mean you want me to take responsibility for pinpointing your delusion?"

"You think I'm delusional?"

"I don't know. If you pretended to believe that you were Jesus in order to be admitted then perhaps you are not delusional. But then of course your motive for coming in here as a patient may be linked to serious disturbance. If you believe you are Jesus and omnipotent then I believe you are delusional." As he said this Steiner felt that this wasn't therapy at all. Indeed, he wondered just what was going on and felt uneasy. He was surely saying too much. Though of course it could be rationalized under the heading of confrontation with reality—what people in the field called "reality testing."

"I'm certainly not omnipotent, Dr. Steiner. God is not omnipotent. God gets tired. God sleeps."

"Then you are in contact with him?"

"If I say yes, then you will surely come to the conclusion that I'm crazy. Isn't that right, Dr. Steiner?

Why does God have to be omnipotent to be God?"

"You're evading the issue."

"Call me Jesus, Dr. Steiner, so that we can put the issue away."

"You mean you prefer I call you Jesus?"

"As you wish."

Neither of them said anything for ten minutes.

Jesus spoke.

"If a person did hear from God—I don't mean an attack of faith or a so-called born-again experience, I mean direct communication—he would automatically be labeled crazy wouldn't he? And if that is the conclusion, then Jesus of Nazareth was either psychotic or a psychopathic manipulator and the world has since been equally psychotic in its beliefs."

Steiner said nothing.

"Then if a messiah or Son of God or prophet—a true prophet—appeared today he'd immediately be called crazy—schizophrenic reaction, paranoid type—right, Dr. Steiner?"

"Probably right."

"Let me ask you something else. Supposing you were dealing with somebody who is delusional, who in fact does project out what he himself thinks and then believes it comes back to him from another source, a higher source. But suppose the substance of what he thinks and projects is valid and even more than valid, wise and useful. Does the fact that he projects it and delusionally feels that it comes from another source make it less valid, or useless, or psychotic?"

"Are you asking me if"—and he chose his next words

carefully—"if disturbed people can have valid ideas, thoughts, theories? Of course they can, and much more. They can also be creative, brilliantly creative."

"Can the substance of their creative brilliance also be the stuff of their projection and sickness?"

"Yes."

"But if their thinking and feeling is valid, really valid, Dr. Steiner, is it possible that this would negate the diagnosis of paranoia and would indicate that in fact they are in touch with an outside source and do not suffer from what psychiatrists call a thought disorder?"

"I suppose that would depend on the beliefs, faith, and credibility of the psychiatric expert in question. His own receptivity or lack of it, to the possibility of the existence of God, let alone a true representative of God on earth, would be all-important."

"And psychiatrists do not usually have that receptivity?"

"Not usually," Steiner said, coolly.

"But perhaps other people do," Jesus said quietly. "They did two thousand years ago and continue in that belief today."

"Perhaps," Steiner said.

Jesus and Mary

"How did you know?" he asked Mary.

"By how I felt when I saw you, when I heard your voice."

"How?" he asked.

"Whole," she said, smiling sweetly. Then after a few minutes of silence she said, "For the first time whole and at peace."

"You were receptive, you had been waiting," he suggested gently.

"Oh yes, that's true. I was more than waiting, I was prepared. I was ready. But only for you. No imposter could be received by me however much I was ready to receive and however much I wanted my wait to end. No one else gave or gives me this feeling, the sense of peace and wholeness."

"And you don't think you are crazy?"

"For the first time in this lifetime of mine I am sane."

"This lifetime?"

"This time is a particle. There is a longer time—a time before and a time after—call it *Forever Time*." He expected these words, his words, his father's words. This only confirmed what he already knew. They were born of the same wisdom.

She went on.

"I was the vehicle of your soul aeons ago. He gave you life through me. Ages before this life he gave you life through me. Your current parents gave you your current body. But we come of him. We are a true trinity. And this happened ages ago. Why did we wait so long? Why has the world waited so long?"

"Because he slept. He slept for two thousand years. He gets tired too. He is not omnipotent. But he is no longer asleep. He is awake now. He is awake to and through me."

Psychiatric Conference

"BUT HE ISN'T SAYING Roma Berlino any more, Dr. Morton, and Frank Bishop knows who he is and is no longer mute. In fact I heard them talking and they sounded perfectly rational. They seemed to be interested in the news and in what was happening in the world generally. They are not preoccupied with themselves."

"What are you trying to tell me, Steiner?"

"Only what I observed. I draw no conclusions at all."

"Thorazine is a very effective drug," Kline said. "Maybe I ought to put my actress on it because she sure as hell is delusional as ever."

"Is she agitated, Kline?" asked Morton testily.

"No. Typical delusional beatitude."

"So we have a miracle performed by a delusional Jesus and Mary," Morton said in a tired voice. "The power of suggestion is stronger than Thorazine, Kline."

"But neither Roma nor Frank knew anything about the Jesus and Mary delusion of the others."

"What did they do?" Morton asked.

"The way I heard it they encouraged them to sound off, to act out," the would-be actress chief nurse said. "You know," she added, "a bit of old-fashioned psychodrama."

"I really think it was something else," Steiner ventured.

"OK, shoot," said Morton, pleasantly now.

"I know this will sound maudlin and clichéd but I think it's caring."

"They showed how they cared?" asked the nurse.

"More than that," Steiner said. "They really did and do care. It can't be faked. It only shows if you feel it and I think they do."

Kline said, "Are you trying to tell me that a pair of paranoid schizophrenics care? How can they care except as a function of their delusion and to further feed their sense of superiority through Christ-like qualities?"

"Their affect is appropriate," Steiner said almost under his breath.

"A lot can go on at the same time," said Morton lightly. Then to Steiner, "Affect is often normal in paranoids."

"Bullshit," responded Kline with a smile.

"You see—you say bullshit as you smile," said Morton. "An example of inappropriate affect."

"You know they've done it several times a day,"
Steiner said, ignoring the interchange between Kline
and Morton. He went on, "They had a larger and larger
circle sounding off Roma Berlino."

"Yes, at one point last Saturday they had the whole
day room involved. I was going to stop them and then
I thought, why?" said the nurse.

"I understand there were some attendants and student nurses singing too," Morton said.

"Also some visitors," Steiner added.

"Jesus said they broke through the Thorazine bar-
rier," Steiner said. He felt odd about revealing anything
that went on in individual sessions with his patient but
also felt that perhaps his patient would be pleased.

"What the hell are we running here?" Kline asked
indignantly. "We should probably up the doses. And
at least for Christ's sake let's stop calling them Jesus
and Mary!"

"Why?" the nurse asked. "And why up the dose?"
No one answered.

"Everyone is livelier since they came," ventured the
social worker.

"It's the caring," Steiner said, thinking, *screw you
Kline* and at the same time feeling surprised at his feeling of loyalty to his patient. *Must watch my countertrans-
ference*, he thought.

"When do you start your own analysis?" Morton
asked Steiner, seemingly out of the blue.

"Not for some time. Classes begin in several weeks
and then the Institute gives us a list of training analysts
to choose from."

"We used to get into analysis right away in the old days," Morton said.

"Are you going to get analytic training?" Morton asked Kline.

"No," Kline said emphatically. "I'll read all the theories but I can't see all that time spent in personal analysis."

The nurse thought briefly of her own personal analysis and how it had been crucial to her survival but she said nothing.

"So you think they really care?" Morton gently reintroduced the subject to Steiner.

"I think they are delusional as hell and have a typical mutual craziness—a *folie à deux*—going and I think caring is part of their delusional goodness thing. But I also think they care." He said this almost defensively at Kline.

"Caring and demonstrating that caring for someone else's needs and style, however crazy or against so-called cultural norms it may be, is a rare thing," Morton stated.

"Well, they sure demonstrated it," the nurse said.

"How?" asked the internist who seemed deep in his own thoughts up to this time.

"By getting them to sound off, to yell, to dance, to join together and not give a damn about what was nice and quiet and supposedly well-behaved." Her face was flushed. "I kind of felt like yelling out Roma Berlino myself." She then fell silent as if embarrassed.

"Maybe you should get rid of them now," Morton almost whispered.

"Rockland State?" Kline asked. "Just sounds like acting out to me."

"Ridiculous," the nurse said.

"There are crazier ones on the street and a lot more dangerous," the nurse said and then added almost despite herself, "Maybe we all need to act out more."

"These two are pretty dangerous," the internist said.

"Yes," Dr. Morton said in a barely audible voice and added, "We'll keep them for the time being."

Steiner felt confused.

Psychotherapy

"THERE'S only one kind of monument worthy of existence."

"What's that?" Steiner asked.

"Each community, town, city, county must build an atrocity monument. The monument must be rendered by a true artist. He will depict the worst atrocity the community has committed."

"So morbid. Is your compassion only reserved for hospitalized patients?" Steiner asked.

"Not at all. I'm suggesting a most compassionate enterprise."

"It sounds less than compassionate—more like punishment," Steiner said gently.

"Facing reality is only temporary punishment. This idea prescribes reality in the service of ultimate compassion. The statues would be constructed to remind people of their own capacity and potential for atrocity."

"What statue would you suggest for us here in our city or county?"

"A mural—a huge mural showing people who are 'different' being constrained and abused."

"Have you witnessed anything like that?" Steiner asked gently.

"Many times. But I will not talk about my past. Indeed, details involving me personally are of no interest."

Some psychotherapy, Steiner thought.

"But perhaps you will tell me this—do you have a capacity and potential for atrocity?"

"Yes," Jesus said emphatically, "and also for grandiosity and omnipotence and pride and self-glorification and competition and selfish detachment—and the struggle for humility which is the greatest struggle of all," he added quietly.

"And God, what of his potential for all this?" Steiner asked.

"God is capable of atrocity, arrogance, vindictive triumph, and all and everything that man is capable of. My Father has the potential of all of his children in all areas of being."

"Your father?" Steiner quickly retorted.

"My Father, your Father, our Father—don't make a

big thing of it, Dr. Steiner. If you want to believe I'm
delusional then you will believe it even without evidence that I feel specially connected to him. If my being
delusional is of lesser importance to you, you will stop
playing detective and judge and we can then meet as
friends."

Labyrinth

IN THE LABYRINTH she told him that she was taking him
to see Henry Salter. He thought, *and my Father said,
cancer abounds*, and he gently said,

"Dr. Henry Salter has been a victim of the species."

"Victim of the species?" she asked.

"Cancer is a man-made construct," he said.

"But I want to see him."

He held her hand and gently said,

"Henry Salter is no longer here."

"How do you know? Did he tell you?"

"I had the thought that *cancer abounds*—these were
his words, my words—and then I had the feeling that
he was no longer here."

"You could be wrong," she said angrily.

"No," he answered firmly.

"Then you could have saved him." She pulled her hand away.

"No," he said firmly and then added, "He was one of society's martyrs—unwillingly and unwittingly—martyrdom is also a man-made construct. But he is saved. He is out of pain."

She wept now and through her tears said, "I wanted you to meet him. I wanted you to save him." Then she wiped her tears. Her mood changed. She took his hand and said very gently,

"Come, this time you are wrong. He is still alive. Come and save him."

"I'm right. This phase is over for him. There are no miracles, only the wisdom of reality and compassion. Salter went back. Miracles are the stuff of lies and selfish liars. But he did not go to a bad or even unfamiliar place. We all go back to where we came from before we arrived here."

"You are lying," she screamed at him. "You are lying." She was hysterical now. "He's alive. He's alive and you can't save him because you're not really Jesus." She suddenly felt panic overwhelm her. A sense of being Betty swept over her—Betty, she thought, but she couldn't remember her second name.

She ran from him and to the tunnel which led to the surgical pavilion, feeling nausea and dizziness sweep over her as she made distance from him.

He called after her, "I don't know my way without you, Mary. I will wait here."

He sat down on the floor and felt grateful for his helplessness. Humility was the most difficult gift to retain and the most valuable gift of all and this blow to her faith and his being lost would help him to retain it.

And he was calm. He sat quietly, totally at peace and waited, hoping that his certainty of her return did not indicate a touch of arrogance to spoil his slight feeling of helplessness.

The Species Goes On

AND she did return.

"You were right," she said.

They said nothing for several minutes.

Then he stood up and hugged her and she wept quietly and then said,

"My faith was shaken. Forgive me." *For such a short time*, he thought.

"You were sorely disappointed," he said, "and like everyone you've had false notions about God. Liars have perpetuated their lies for centuries. God has no interest in miracles. Praying has no meaning."

"Forgive me," she pleaded.

"There is nothing to forgive," he said. "We are part of his unity and wisdom as ever."

Then he took her hand and said, "Take me to the

place where the newborn babies are shown." And she did.

There were some relatives looking through the glass at infants, some of them born only hours earlier.

They looked too and nobody noticed them or heard when he said, "Perhaps that little husky boy over there, the serious looking one, will be your friend."

"A new Henry Salter," she said and smiled as they headed back to their wing.

"The species goes on," he said.

Therapy

"GOD gives life. He doesn't destroy. He creates. He doesn't terminate. He does not function in relation to any morality system contrived by man, let alone by schemers."

"Schemers?" Steiner questioned.

"Those (and he recalled his father's message after his two-thousand-year sleep) who tell people how evil ordinary components of the human condition are, in order to exert power over them. Schemers deny ordinary pleasures in his name, so as to be in the all-powerful position of absolving them from sins, which are no sins at all, when pleasure is experienced."

"Then what are the sins?"

"Being human is no sin. But death-dealing instruments include competition, selfish isolation, glory seeking, power, prestige, and the sociopathic society and its whole hooray-for-me—the-hell-with-you philosophy. A philosophy of death. Death by war, by a thousand pollutions, by cancer. Beware perfection and greatness. What can I say of a culture in which cancer is sold and promoted and nationalized for a profit?" Steiner thought about the advertising and the sale of tobacco while people are *protected* against sexual excess in all the media of the world.

"But why didn't God make man more virtuous?" Steiner asked.

"And risk the death of free choice? And make automatons and clones? No. Without free choice man would no longer be man. God gave life and man must decide whether he will use this primitive form he is in to evolve further so that perhaps one day he will be out of danger of extinction. Otherwise he will stagnate, then regress. Man must decide the issue. Will it be one of encapsulated selfishness, ultimate self-corrosion, and species extinction, or of cooperation and evolvement? *This now*, this point in the species' existence, is only one step along the way of his potential evolution. God gave him the potential but will not make the choice. Man is man because God did not take away his choice of destiny when he created him."

"Then it is pointless to pray?" Steiner suggested.

"The Jews pray for greater self-understanding and sometimes God responds and makes us partners of his wisdom. Though self-awareness has not protected them from their brothers and sisters."

"Brothers and sisters?" Steiner questioned.

"There is no hope for the species, none, if any group is singled out or separated out for any reason at all. In cancer, one group of cells annihilates another group and the body dies. The species will live or die accordingly."

"The original Jesus was a Jew," Steiner said.

"That is why Jews have been persecuted. Not because they killed him. They didn't. But because they produced him. People can't tolerate the presence of people who produced God—a punitive God—and then seem to escape from his rule themselves."

"Punitive?" Steiner questioned.

"His interpreters gave them rules they cannot live up to and dictums which produce self-revulsion. They project this onto Jews, believing that Jews escaped the dictums and are free.

And what about you? Steiner thought.

Request

HE LIKED the progress Steiner was making. He felt that Steiner was partaking more and more in the wisdom of the unity, as he came to call it. He liked Steiner's questions. He felt that Steiner had become less bound to the idea of psychotherapy and more interested in sharing important concepts. This was good.

He thought that Steiner was becoming increasingly open and, on a feeling level, was probably experiencing greater self-acceptance and acceptence of the human condition. Steiner quite readily agreed with him that the species was in an interim stage and light-years away from its potential development. He also readily realized that no highly evolved stage could be reached if the species destroyed itself during any interim. Each *now* is a link to the future and rupture of a single link obliterates the future. He and Steiner agreed that the entire species constituted a complete organism and that the organism could not survive if it attacked and digested parts of itself.

And then he asked Steiner if he would ask Morton to eliminate Thorazine and all other tranquilizers, sedatives, hypnotics, and energizers from the division, or at least dilute them.

Thorazine

"THEY ARE better. Just about all of them are better. Since they've been here we've discharged quite a number."

"We always discharge quite a number, Steiner." They were alone in Dr. Morton's office.

"Yes, Dr. Morton, but these people were in better shape, really better shape, not a drug-induced better shape."

"Are you suggesting a miracle, Steiner?" Morton asked pleasantly.

"No." He felt embarrassed.

"Might it be a good thing for your own analysis to begin soon?" Morton questioned gently.

"Are you trying to tell me something, Dr. Morton?"

"People who work in these places should all be in analysis." He said this with considerable conviction.

"I was just thinking, what if we stopped drugs or used them a lot less?" Steiner responded.

"Steiner, is that your idea or his?" Morton asked dryly.

"His?"

"His, him, your delusional Jesus. Be careful of entering a delusion. People have been known to be sucked in and then not been able to get out."

"Sucked in?"

"Yes, a *folie à deux* can become *trois* or a hundred. Look at Hitler's Germany."

"Look at Christianity," Steiner said.

"Anyway, people, even seasoned therapists, have been known to be seduced into believing delusional patients—thus becoming part of the delusional system themselves."

"And becoming delusional?" Steiner asked.

"Yes," Morton replied with fatigue.

"But I thought a delusion or any form of thought disorder as part of a psychotic process was always years in the making. You said that even an encapsulated delusion represented a malignant process eventually involving the whole personality." Steiner felt better. He thought he had countered well.

"True, but also true that some of us are unaware of unconscious processes which have been years in the making, and in which potential can be made kinetic by events unforeseen in the past."

"So you are saying we don't know who has a proclivity for craziness," Steiner asked politely.

"I'm saying that and more. I'm also saying there's a lot we don't know."

"But what if Jesus of Nazareth—Christ—was not crazy? What if he turned up and was here now? Would we give him Thorazine?"

"Probably. Be careful, Steiner!"

"Careful?"

"Yes, and perhaps it's time to discharge him and her too. They could certainly get along outside," Morton said quietly.

"Maybe they'd be even more dangerous outside—I mean to the public at large," Steiner said evenly.

"You're angry. I won't discharge them—yet—but I can't do away with Thorazine. You can lower the doses and even stop them on select cases. But take it easy. Keep in mind this guy may be brilliant but he's crazy. Also, keep in mind that patients have been known to help other patients. In fact it's a common occurrence. Look at AA, Gamblers Anonymous, Overeaters Anonymous, and all those buddy systems. See you around."

Steiner felt dismissed and left the office, marveling at how Morton could mention copatient organizations in this connection. His last remarks seemed trite, simplistic, and even inappropriate. Morton was a more profound man than that and Steiner felt disappointed. *Compassionate father figures are hard to come by*, he laughed to himself. And then he thought that Morton's remark was really defensive. *Yes*, he thought, *Morton was defensive*.

Ring-Around-a-Rosy

"EVEN AS I tell you that sociopathy and all forms of legal gangsterism must be eradicated, it won't be done by force, only by compassion. Look here on these wards or anywhere—the people who need love the most are the least lovable. The arrogant, the vindictive, the ones without conscience, the criminal, the ruthless—punishment does not help and justice is a contrived expedient."

"In defense of the sick among us whom we hate," Steiner said dryly.

"When we hate them, we hate, repress, and in so doing make more powerful those same aspects in ourselves."

"Then love will cure all?" Steiner asked.

"Clichéd, I know, but true nevertheless," Jesus smiled. "The task is not easy. It requires much struggle in a society whose key words are glory, greatness, and perfection, in a society which fattens and kills Earth's most innocent creatures so that tender meat may be served to those who can afford it, in a culture that kills whales and seals and of course its own members."

"And you intend to change all this?" Steiner asked.

"Compassion is infectious. Look at the ward, at the day room."

"What do you really think happens among the patients in the day room?"

"You mean how do we do it—Mary and me?"

"Yes, how?" Steiner asked. "To what do you attribute your success?" he added for no reason other than he somehow felt put down.

"We play ring-around-a-rosy," Jesus said with utmost seriousness and then added, "Do you know the game?"

"Yes—I do," Steiner replied. He felt a little silly but he said, "Ring-around-a-rosy, a pocket full of posies, ashes, ashes, we all fall down."

"Yes, you know it alright. Children have a naiveté linked to a kind of species wisdom passed on from generation to generation and obliterated by adult cynicism. In this game we get some of this back. We hold hands and there's a feeling-communication which takes place among us. We dance in a circle and feel a sense of cooperation. And some of us fall down and this reminds us of the value of humility. And we sing out—we sing out what we feel, what we are, ignoring all demands and niceties and in these moments we are ourselves even as we are together and know that ashes are also part of the larger universe."

After a long silence Steiner asked almost as an afterthought, "Do you believe in life after death?"

"It doesn't concern me," he answered. "Life during life concerns me."

Roma Berlino

ROMA BERLINO was brought back to the hospital seventeen days after he left. He was in a catatonic stupor, rigid and mute. Drug intervention did not help. After feeding him through a stomach tube for two days, the staff decided to give him a series of six electrosubconvulsive treatments. This made him slightly less rigid but there was no appreciable improvement. Tube-feeding continued. The staff discussed certification and transfer to one of the state hospitals. But Steiner interceded with Morton and this was delayed.

Nobody interfered with the ring-around-a-rosy exercises in the day room and an appreciable drop in drug therapy took place. It became evident to Steiner that Jesus and Mary spent considerable time with each patient. They talked to some and just sat silently with others, sometimes for hours. Mary hugged and kissed a few.

Roma was in an isolation room.

Conversation

"HIS EXPLANATION for anti-Semitism makes sense."

"Steiner, a lot of what paranoids say makes sense," Morton said gently and patiently.

"Why not let them see him—Roma? It might be an interesting experiment."

"You really have a vested interest in believing he's something special."

Steiner ignored the remark.

"Nobody had been able to reach him. ECT hasn't worked. What's to lose?" he pleaded.

"Alright, let them. But you will either be disappointed or further sucked in by their machinations."

"Machinations—they've certainly done no harm. And they have helped—you know that."

"I know that harm sometimes comes in strange ways," the older man replied.

A Man Dies

ROMA BERLINO came out of his stupor and began talking again three days after Jesus and Mary started sitting with him. They never left his side. They were nearly always both there and at least one of them was always with him. Some of the staff attributed his remission to them. Some said it was pure coincidence.

On the seventh day Roma Berlino found a few moments alone and a razor blade and during the night cut his throat and bled to death.

Nearly everybody on the staff said and believed that his suicide was inevitable.

But Jesus felt otherwise.

Self-hate

"I was instrumental in his death. Indeed I may have killed him."

He lay on his bed trembling. Periodically his teeth chattered.

"You did not!" Mary said firmly.

"I cannot absolve myself of the responsibility." His eyes filled with tears. He shuddered and began to shake violently.

"Dr. Steiner told me to remind you of what you said: That nothing and nobody in this universe—not even God—is omnipotent."

"Your faith may have been misplaced," he said in a very low voice.

"My faith was and is well-placed!" she said with great authority.

"Perhaps I am a false prophet. I have duped myself and you. I am not his son. I am a fraud."

"You are his son!"

"Please sleep now."

And finally he did.

The Message

AND God's voice thundered:
    "Omnipotence does not exist.
    "No martyrdom!
    "Do not suffer for them!
    "Do not die for them!
    "Live for them!
    "The way to me is not through death but through life.
    "Man is man and man has choice.
    "Even the most desperate choose.
    "Your lessons in the cauldron were good.
    "Your lessons in humility will serve you well.
    "The rehearsal is over!
    "Go with Mary into the world!"

Discharge

"THEY'VE ASKED to be discharged."
    "I know," Steiner replied.
    "There's no reason to hold them back," Morton said.

"I know," said Steiner.

"They seem in very good shape."

"I know," Steiner said again. "Do you think the catatonic stupor protected him—Roma—from his own self-hate—from murdering himself?" Steiner asked in a very low voice.

"I don't know," Morton answered quietly. "But I do know they've helped a lot of people. However they did it, they did it. They won't be alone out there. I'm sure some of the people we've discharged are already waiting for them."

He patted Steiner on the shoulder as he saw him to the door and said,

"You know he's going out a mystery—we never did find out who he really is or where he came from."

"I know," said Steiner, leaving the room.

FOUR

God requires no synagogue—except in
the heart.
                    —Hasidic saying

Rebirth

THE SUN was shining brightly. It was the beginning of winter again but there was no evidence of winter's birth.

Everything had a clean, bright, spring look.

After they had walked a considerable distance they both had the same impulse. They turned and waved good-bye to the building. And they noticed someone waving at them and running toward them. He thought it looked like Steiner.

FIVE

Hospitality to strangers shows reverence for the name of the Lord.
> —*Talmud: Shabbath, 127a*

Welcome everyone—with joy.
> —*Saying of the Fathers, 1:15*

The Place

THEY WALKED through streets. She held his hand and they walked for many miles, crisscrossing some areas again and again.

To an interested observer it would have seemed like purposeless and even confused, wasted motion.

But this was a reacquaintance and reassessment exploration. This was their way of receiving the important sights, sounds, and smells, and evaluating them.

Nothing had changed. People were miserable. Some were happy. There were the ruthless ones—and the caring ones. Some were ragged, tired, hungry, lost. Some were cold and getting colder as darkness came. Some were catatonic. It was a macrocosm of the hospital.

He felt apprehensive. He waited for his father's message. None came. He held Mary's hand and felt more substantial.

She had not felt so light in years. Without the bags and packs she used to carry, she felt that she could jump and float in the air.

And then when he was cold and tired she led him to a small obscure street in the lower part of the city and took a key from the little bag she carried and unlocked the door of a small, strange building which years earlier had been converted to an off-off-off Broadway theater and rehearsal hall. It had been abandoned and forgotten for years. A friend from a distant time and life had lent or given her the place. It was an odd place—with many rooms scattered above and around a moderate-sized auditorium.

The Search for the Mirror

IT HAD BEEN out of sight and memory for days.

But the need brought it to mind and to existence and to powerfully wanting it. He would not leave the place without it.

He ran from one room to the other, to a few tiny rooms off the stage that he liked to sit and dream in. He scurried up and down the moderate-sized stage, through the rows of folding chairs—but there was no clue. The mirror sent him no message—nothing at all. *Did I ever have it?* he thought. *Is it part of a dream? Am I dreaming now?* Separating dream from reality became almost as important as the mirror. Mary would help him. She seemed to be able to find anything—in the hospital, the place, the streets, anywhere.

But she was out buying food. She also sustained the miracle of money—actually from a small trust also of another life and time.

He couldn't wait. But the mirror sent no message.

Was it a dream—the chests of drawers, the rows of seats, the stage, the closets, the rooms, the place itself? "No!" he said out loud. "This is not a dream!" he shouted. "I am here and Mary will be here and this place is this place and the mirror exists." But he wasn't at all sure. The mirror itself would validate reality so that his need for it now became desperate.

Then his search became more frenetic. He threw clothes on the beds and looked behind the pillows of the worn-out old couches and under the auditorium chairs and then he suddenly stopped and very slowly and quietly walked to the center of the stage and stood absolutely still as he looked out over the semidark theater.

He emptied his mind and then thought: *Father, help me find it—your gift to me—help me now.*

And then he heard God's voice and he knew this was not a dream.

"Sit," it said. "Sit and be calm, my son."

He sat on a folding chair in the middle of the almost-dark stage. God's voice filled his mind.

"The mirror will manifest itself to you. Empty your mind and join mine." And he did.

And when he heard God's voice he knew this was not a dream.

"Sit," it said. "Sit and be at peace, my son."

He sat center stage on the chair for more than an hour. His eyes focused on the empty seats of the theater and remained on them, fixed and unblinking. In his mind's eye the seats filled with people—all kinds—small, large, poor, rich, sad, happy, sick, vital—and he knew that he was looking into the future even as his mind remained free of word thoughts.

And then rigidity became utter relaxation and even more than relaxation. He floated up from the chair as his soul—God's soul—moved him to the smallest room off the stage. And on the small table where he was certain it had not been before was the four-by-five-inch oak-framed mirror. Mary had found it in a village antique store years earlier.

The Mirror

HE SAT on the chair and, holding the mirror with both hands framing the frame, he saw his face in it. And then with combined willpower, faith, and hope his face left the mirror and it cleared, reflecting nothing at all.

Now he saw Mary in the mirror. She was two streets away, carrying three large paper shopping bags. The street was crowded with people and her progress was slow and labored.

He concentrated on the people and they moved away and left the street so that only she remained. He kept the streets clear so that she could walk quickly.

And as she reached the theater door his face returned to the mirror again and he went to the entrance of the building and greeted her.

The Attack

THAT NIGHT Mary had a terrible dream in which she was being smothered. Walls moved in on her and heavy weights crushed her chest.

She managed to scream herself awake with what little breath was left her and then the attack began in full force. She couldn't breathe fast enough and as she tried her heart raced out of control.

And he did not have to be called.

In his dream he heard her and he was in her small room and held her hand as she woke from her dream and her anxiety grew.

"Picture your terror as a solid mass filling your being," he told her quietly. And she did.

"Now we are going to wall it off and contract it," he told her. "What color is it?" he suddenly asked.

"Gray," she shot back.

"Yes, it's always gray," he said. "Now bring it down in size in the picture of it in your mind."

"Yes," she complied.

"Now put strong walls—pure white walls—around it."

"Yes," she complied. The hyperventilation had stopped. Her heart no longer raced.

"Now bring the walls together."

"Yes," she said.

"Squeeze the mass and grayness out of existence."

"Yes," she said.

"Now let the walls go back to where they came from." She did and she fell asleep and dreamed of green fields and the smell of cut grass. The anxiety attack was over.

He returned to his room and bed and relinquished his mind-picture of green fields as he drifted into a dreamless sleep.

Steiner

THEY BOTH stared at the mirror.

She saw them both looking back at them. The mirror never cleared for her. She could only close her eyes and imagine what he described.

Now the mirror was clear—no reflections.

And then Steiner suddenly appeared—thoroughly surprising and startling him.

"It's Steiner," he told her.

He looked closely. Steiner was in tears, distraught. Clearly, something terrible had happened to him. Jesus knew at once.

"Someone died," he told Mary. "Steiner has lost a loved one."

"I'll take you to him," Mary said.

The Visit

THEY SAT in his office waiting for him to speak.

"I lost her."

"That is why we are here."

"She died instantly. Never saw the car."

They said nothing.

"She was all I had. Two months ago. Now it is worse than ever. It all turned black for me—the entire world."

"Gray," Mary said.

Steiner smiled through his tears—the first smile in two months.

"We met when I was eighteen. She was sixteen."

Steiner looked awful—gaunt, unshaven, black hollows under his eyes.

"Come with us," Jesus said.

"We will eat on the barrel," Mary said.

"Eat on the barrel." Steiner smiled again. "I remember eating on the barrel whenever we moved."

"I know," Mary said.

"Gray—yes gray—not black," Steiner burst out and then began to sob.

When he stopped he looked at them quizzically.

Jesus said, "You are thinking about how you can reveal yourself to two psychotics. Can you forget we are crazy for just a while?—put it aside! Come with us. Let us help you."

"Help me with what?"

"To find peace."

On the Barrel

IT WAS gray and very cold outside but not in the place.

There were no stage lights or house lights either. But there was plenty of heat and many lamps of all descriptions all over the building. Mary liked to keep the place warm and bright.

There were barrels in the place and several of them were on the stage. Mary had bought a load of food at Katz's and they spread it out on the barrels.

Mary had bought much more than they could possibly eat.

Bread—all kinds—pastrami, corned beef, hot dogs, chicken salami, coleslaw, sauerkraut, potato salad, french fries, kosher pickles, beer, soft drinks, cake—four varieties—tea, coffee—and Steiner ate with a huge appetite for the first time in weeks. And he had the thought: *Manic supply of food—manic eating*, and he felt like an ingrate and also guilty.

"You're wondering if you are allowed to feel better," Jesus said to him gently.

Steiner smiled.

"First, how can a psychotic, delusional young man make you feel better? And then, are you permitted to feel better after such a terrible loss?"

Steiner's thought was how capable schizophrenics are at being able to discern other people's feelings.

"You are thinking I know what you feel because my ego boundaries are so fluid I can virtually cross over into your skin. But couldn't this ability also be part of healthy empathy? Besides, your feeling better because of me doesn't make you crazy or less expert at what you do—so why defend against it?"

Steiner said nothing.

"I wonder how many people saw Christ, the two-thousand-year-ago version, as psychotic?" Mary said.

"I lost her only two months ago," Steiner said, thinking, *I'll never stop being depressed.*

"But you will," Jesus said.

"I will what?" Steiner asked.

"Your mood will change. There is no sin in its changing now—right now. Don't you see?—life is everything—and joy is life."

Steiner marveled at how he felt better—too good to talk. For the first time, he noted his surroundings—a strange place.

Jesus said,

"Don't hate yourself later on for feeling better now—take time off from your current mood. And of course expect your doubts about us to return.

"But let me ask you how many schizophrenics you have met who can empathize and emotionally invest in other people?"

Steiner did not reply.

"Of course you can say that my kind of relating is part of my delusion and therefore not a function of real feelings at all. Besides, you know of many people who are quite sane outside of their encapsulated delusion where their insanity takes place."

That was exactly what Steiner thought.

"But I feel at peace," Steiner said spontaneously, without connection to what he was thinking.

"Yes," replied Mary.

The Children

ON THE WAY back to Steiner's office he noticed the posters on the lampposts. They were pictures of small children missing from their parents' homes for weeks, some even for many years. He studied them as tears ran down his cheeks and he held Mary's hand tightly.

Steiner seemed happier.

"My delusion is an updated one," Jesus told him.

"How so?" Steiner asked.

"The universe is God and it—he—communicates through me." But then a frown came over his face.

"What's the matter?" Steiner asked. Mary took her son's hand in hers.

"I thought of times when I do feel as if dissolution of myself is taking place. Going crazy to you perhaps. A panic attack in technical terms. This happens when I have a sense of the cosmos. The enormity of it and all that it contains is suddenly there and I am over-whelmed."

"I guess we all experience it more or less at times. Existential anxiety."

"No, Dr. Steiner—it's more that that." Now he leaned closer and confided, "You see, at those times I feel, I believe, that I as a self am ending and that I'm being dissolved into fragments which will be absorbed by the universe."

And then I will be part of it—but as a nonself I will be the cosmos itself—part of God in purest form. At those times I feel frightened but quite sane, yet I know that you would consider it the height of megalomania."

"Or humility," Steiner replied.

Audiences

THE DOOR was unlocked and people drifted in.

They sat on the folding chairs and Mary gave them food.

Some ate. Some didn't.

There was a woman who wore a beautiful fur coat and a heady perfume. She did not eat.

One man, an insomniac, sat and slept deeply.

An exhausted young woman and her rambunctious one-year-old wandered in and sat. She had a cup of hot tea.

Two adolescent black boys came in for a while, left, returned, and then sat and watched very quietly.

There was a very old man in a wheelchair.

A heavy old woman, a former professional dancer, came in and seemed restless.

There were others.

Steiner came.

Some stayed. Some left. A few slept over. Many returned. Others never came back. Some returned with other people.

Laughing

Jesus pointed to Mary and she laughed. Mary pointed to Jesus and he laughed. Then they laughed together and encouraged the audience to laugh.

Soon they all laughed—some until tears rolled down their cheeks.

Jesus then told them that they had all had an experience in joy.

He then sat and Mary did too and everyone was silent. He then said to them again that they had had an experience in joy.

The dancer and an adolescent came up on the stage and played the laughing game and once again everyone laughed.

Later on Steiner sat with Jesus in a small room as Mary talked with some of the people who remained and asked them about their lives.

"You now have a church," Steiner said.

"A church is a theater," replied Jesus, "and this theater is a theater of joy. How do you feel?"

"Good," said Steiner.

"You see, this is not a theater of the absurd—or perhaps it is but no more than churches are."

"Laughing is contagious."

"And better than praying," Jesus said. "Praying reminds me of preying—preying on God—asking—demanding—cajoling."

"Praying is a form of connection, to him, to all of us," Steiner said, feeling rather pretentious.

"Laughing is better—innocent," Jesus replied.

"Not all laughing," Steiner said.

"Derisive cackling is not laughing. The real thing is truly sacred and one of God's greatest gifts to man."

Dancing

AND it came to pass that they danced. First there was only music. Mary had somehow produced a cassette recorder and a variety of tapes. But one day the dancer became inspired. She did it. And then she got the others to do it too. Twenty-seven people including their hosts danced.

She got them all on the stage and they even got the wheelchair up there. And they all moved about. It was disjointed but it was a kind of dancing. They had varying degrees of fun. Some really let go and felt joyous for a sustained time. This was often followed by a period of long, deep peace. Some of them without sharing their thoughts had the fleeting notion that he truly was a prince of peace.

And they danced all kinds of dances—moving about

in different ways, sometimes to the music and as often oblivious to it.

But the dancer never lost patience. She tried again and again to pattern them into a single unit. Sometimes they only did it for a short time. Jesus did not interfere. They did not play ring-around-a-rosy.

When Steiner was there he did not participate and yet he did. He saw himself as an observer. But they felt him as an audience. Though no one noticed the dancer had more success with integrating them when Steiner was there.

Any Day

THE PLACE was warm and bright. A few people ate and talked about inconsequential things. The mirror reflected the city streets and more. It was very cold and a wet snow made the streets wet.

The air was full of poisonous fumes, mainly exhaust from idling buses and truck diesel engines.

A fire destroyed six houses, nearly killing three children and leaving fourteen adults and seven children homeless, but no one died.

Three sewer covers exploded into the air. Three people were hurt. No one was killed.

Two men screamed at each other over a parking place but they didn't come to blows.

A mugger stabbed a reluctant client but the client lived.

A woman sat on a store doorstep and smoked a cigarette and shivered now and then. He could not make out her features, which were covered by many layers of grime. Her legs were black with filth. He thought of Mary and he shivered.

He ran into the street. He couldn't find her. But he found a demented, filthy man and Jesus washed him and fed him and then the man ran back to the streets.

The mirror also took him inside of buildings.

Cool, collected, well-dressed men met at the UN and discussed famine, war, nuclear destruction. He could tell that some thought of where to eat that night. One man's thoughts were full of fantasies of whom to sleep with.

There were rich people who thought they were poor, poor people who thought they were rich, and people who didn't think about money at all.

He saw a man getting a haircut and for some reason this made him anxious but the scene changed quickly.

Some teenagers sat around on the floor of a small room playing guitars and singing.

A man and a woman spoke of their love for each other.

A woman washed and powdered a baby boy.

The mirror switched to the streets again.

Two boys walked about, oblivious to the bad weather.

Two lovers kissed, hugged, parted, and then re-

dence to establish a diagnosis of paranoid schizophrenia?"

"Now *you* are becoming psychiatric."

"Entering *your* delusion," Jesus smiled. "Going further into it—isn't a thought disorder required for the diagnosis?"

"A delusion of major proportion is a thought disorder," Steiner replied.

"But a delusion is a delusion only if it is a delusion. Are we arrogant if we ascribe to ourselves that which is actually so?"

"What about the scores of people we see in hospitals, all of whom say they are God or his son or Jesus?"

"Some are and some aren't," Jesus smiled. "Depends what they are feeling, believing, saying, doing, and effecting. God is the cosmos. We are all God. His force is concentrated through us—through some more than others. Some of us are more perceptive than others."

"Who?" Steiner asked.

"Those of us whose perception is not clouded by harsh judgment, affectation, and self-glorification."

They remained silent for a moment and then Jesus said, "Even the cosmos is limited. God is limited. But his consciousness is expanding."

"All of it here on this small planet, through you and others?" Steiner added.

"Wherever the cosmos exists. But our concerns —yours and mine—are appropriate for here and now."

At least he's sharing some of his omnipotence, Steiner thought.

This is a form of joy for him, Jesus thought.

More Visitors

THEY LIVED in the Village and often walked on streets at night that were fairly desolate and a considerable distance from their loft.

Her mother lived with them now and so they were able to take their walks while the older woman sat with their nine-year-old son.

For more than a year after their three-year-old daughter disappeared they went nowhere. She had been paralyzed with depression. They had both been terrified of leaving their small boy out of their sight. At that time he plunged even deeper into his work as an architect. She, a fine artist, stopped painting. But he insisted on bringing her mother to live with them and their walks began. Now, emptiness and a dull ache replaced her depression and terror. He remained enraged and withdrawn.

When they came upon the place she was thirty-seven, he was thirty-nine. Mindy had been gone for three years.

They nearly missed the place. The music late at night attracted him.

She did not want to go in. He did. She complied. Her compliance had become commonplace in the last three years.

They watched the proceedings on the stage: the laughing, the dancing, the eating. They had no desire to participate.

But Mary insisted and they drank hot tea.

They only stayed a short time. And then a real miracle occurred that she barely noticed. She liked his features—the man who seemed to lead them. She hadn't liked anything in years. He took notice of them.

Return

THEY CAME BACK a week later.

She felt urged to paint his portrait.

She began that night.

They both dreamed of Mindy but did not share their dream in the morning.

A dying man spoke to him and said he was afraid.

Jesus said:

"Consciousness ends and sweet infinity begins."

Search

MARY spent much time buying food. He did not go with her. She also bought warm clothes for people. Money came in regularly now. A few pennies from poor people, many dollars from others, large sums from a rich man and a rich woman who showed up now and then.

Several people were always there now.

He searched the streets for the person who needed him. The mirror had been vague for days. But he felt the need—the person's and his own.

A week went by this way and he searched in vain but the mirror reflected the words, *Someone needs you*, and he was restless.

Then one late afternoon on an unusually warm and pleasant day he saw a crowd of people and he knew his search was over.

They were gathered around a thin, well-dressed teenager convulsing on the sidewalk. He didn't seem to be breathing and his color was turning increasingly dark.

Someone asked if there was a doctor in the crowd. No one responded. A woman ran off to find a telephone to call for an ambulance.

Jesus walked through the crowd and knelt beside the boy. He forced the boy's mouth open and asked for a stick. A man gave him a pencil and he put it between the boy's teeth, protecting his tongue.

Jesus held the boy's head out of the gutter with one hand and his forehead with the other.

The boy stopped convulsing. He started to breathe. Color returned to his face.

Two people recognized Jesus and as he disappeared through the crowd they accompanied him back to the place.

For the moment his restlessness was over.

The mirror reflected the streets again that night.

The Pride Imperative

"PREACH? Why would I preach? I'm not looking for narcissistic supplies."

"To help them see the light."

"You are feeling better?"

"Yes, I miss her painfully—all the time. But I feel better."

"Did anyone preach to you?"

"No."

"Preaching can be very destructive. It gives people more rules to comply with. More attempts at self-idealization. More put-down of joy. The preacher who has people rolling, dancing, singing, who is joy-producing—without hysteria, without self-serving designs,

THEODORE ISAAC RUBIN, M.D.

without investment of pride in this or that way of living or behaving—now *that* is a man of God."

Then he said,

"Look at these men at the UN. Aren't they all preachers? They don't struggle for mutual acceptance. Mutual acceptance is not even on their agenda. They fight. What are they fighting for? They are not fighting for territory. They fight for power over people in those territories. They fight to sustain their pride—pride in their method of government, in their culture, in their values, in their religion, in their genes. They are all dictated to by a primitive pride imperative—pride that shields them from terrible feelings of inadequacy. Pride which, when hurt, puts them in touch with their feelings of inadequacy, largely born of lack of humility and lack of acceptance of human limitations. And when their pride is breached, the enormous self-hate they feel is projected out to their neighbors. You only have to look at their faces."

"Have you?" Steiner asked. "I see no television set here."

Jesus sighed. "Through my mirror."

"Mirror?"

"Yes," and he showed Steiner the mirror and how he used it.

"Don't you see how you project your own visions to the mirror?" Steiner asked gently.

"Does it really matter? Isn't the validity of what I see more important than whether or not it is a projection?" Jesus said this with great patience.

The Strike

HE WALKED uptown. He saw a man walking with a small girl. He followed them.

This was the time of the great hotel strike.

The pickets marched up and down in front of the hotel entrances shouting encouraging slogans to each other. They were men and women of various colors and shapes but all dressed poorly.

Two young men passed by, both blond, pressed and dressed in impeccable, expensive clothes. They carried briefcases.

Jesus heard one say to the other,

"Listen to those morons. If I had a machine-gun I'd mow them down." The other laughed and agreed.

Jesus felt sorry for them. They both tripped, fell head-on, and tore their clothes. Their briefcase papers scattered over the sidewalk.

Two pickets helped them to their feet. Two others helped them gather their open briefcases and papers.

They thanked the pickets profusely.

Jesus smiled and walked on. He lost sight of the man and child he had been following.

The Enabler

"Isn't every mother an enabler?" Mary asked.

She went on before Steiner could reply.

"I see myself as an enabler. When I was an actress I sought narcissistic gratification or supplies—*narcissistic supplies*, my son calls it. And I got them. I became a bit of a star, you know."

"A considerable star," Steiner commented.

She ignored the remark and went on.

"Then it revolted me. I don't know how it happened. I saw a therapist for quite a while. Did you know that?"

"No," Steiner replied.

"He believed I was afraid of toppling from the pinnacle and that my revulsion for it all was a self-protective device to prevent disappointment."

"Sour grapes in advance," Steiner said dryly.

"Exactly. But his belief didn't change my revulsion."

"What did you believe?" Steiner asked.

"I felt a dying and a rebelling going on in me. I believe now—and I came to this with his help—that I had become so full of myself, my consciousness, my little insane world, my sycophants, disciples, and support systems that I felt poisoned. I had to take to the streets and one day I was there—a street person. I had to divest myself. I had to be free of it all—to cleanse, to purify—to be born-again—a cliché but true."

"But why the bags in the streets—the bags of things you loaded yourself down with?"

"Residuals and supports of the past. Jesus says that the whole period represented an identity crisis and I still needed things to hold on to, some feeling for who I was during the transitional period—the period between the old life and now. The streets were a transitional time for me. I know that now."

"How did it feel on the streets?"

"My son thinks it all happened gradually, but to me it felt sudden. It was frightening and then it was safe and it gave me peace. I got rid of it all—of every one."

Of all emotional investments, responsibilities, coercions, contracts, Steiner thought.

"I felt free."

"Except for the bags."

"Yes, I needed those. I still didn't know who I was. They kept me from getting too anxious."

"Now?"

"Now I find peace through him—my son," she said.

And glory too, Steiner thought, *and narcissistic supplies too.*

"You call him your son." Steiner felt he was taking considerable risk and would incite great rage in her but he dared to go on. Indeed he felt pushed to go on.

"You know you didn't give birth to him."

But she remained calm.

"I am constantly giving birth to him. His growth is a continuing birth in which I participate. As I told you, I am an enabler. Being an enabler, giving sustenance—love—is real motherhood."

"But you didn't give physical birth to him," Steiner insisted. "In fact had you not been pushed together in the hospital you never would have known him."

"How naive you are," she laughed. "None of it was accidental."

She hesitated a minute and then went on gently,

"You, the others, the hospital, were largely there—mainly there and perhaps only there so that our union would take place."

She waited. Steiner said nothing—actually too overwhelmed by her megalomania and boundless grandiosity. Then she went on good-naturedly.

"Physical birth. How literal and concrete you are. The concrete facts of motherhood are of no importance. Indeed, lack of that bit of nonsense establishes me as a virgin mother. I am his mother through the deepest emotional tie. I continue to be his mother. I shall always be his mother. I am his enabler. He made me well. I help him to make others well—even you. As a psychiatrist, you surely know that if we remove pride, does it matter who gives birth to whom? Don't we then become the parents of all of us?"

Before he could reply she added, "Literal crucifixion means nothing either."

Steiner thought, *Tell that to the person being crucified.*

As a seeming afterthought she said,

"He is crucified whenever anyone suffers."

Peculiarly, Steiner felt very warm toward her even as he thought, *She is an enabler. He experiences most of his insanity through her freeing him to be fairly sane. A very special folie à deux.* But he still felt warm—even loving—

toward her. And as he left the place that evening he had the fleeting crazy ego-alien thought—*Maybe I too would like a mother like that—envy?*

The Unthinkable

FOUR PEOPLE who had been in the hospital drifted in. Somehow they had heard and it gave them great comfort to be reunited.

Indeed, to celebrate, the six of them played the old ring-around-a-rosy game and enjoyed it.

But one young man remained troubled. He told Jesus that he could not drive terrible thoughts from his mind.

Jesus said, "Think the unthinkable and if that doesn't help then the unthinkable hasn't been unthinkable enough and you must think beyond it to the even more unthinkable and do what is thinkable."

The young man thought of his mother dying. He thought of his stabbing her. He thought of his dismembering her. He shuddered but then felt better. He telephoned her and said hello and asked how she was. She hadn't heard from him in two years.

He repeated this process each time his thoughts

became obsessive. He sought out the unthinkable but did only what was thinkable.

No Name

AMONG the well-to-do people one rich man arrived in a limousine from time to time.

He gave Mary five hundred dollars each time he came.

She asked for his name.

"No name," he said and usually left after fifteen minutes of sitting quietly in the audience section of the auditorium.

Notoriety

ONE DAY a young woman came who wanted to do a story about them for a famous magazine. She was especially interested in Mary.

Mary tried to persuade her not to do it but did not succeed.

Fortunately, No Name was there. He took the young woman aside. After he spoke to her she agreed not to do the story.

But she returned and even partook of the dancer's activities on the stage on several occasions.

She became known to Mary as *Notoriety* and Jesus said she had been contained.

Portrait

SHE SHOWED HIM the painting of himself. It was signed "Emily Morrison."

Was he that sensitive, he asked himself?

Was he that vulnerable? To their hurts, not to his own, he told himself. Theirs were his, he told himself.

Was he that benevolent? That disturbed? He did not answer himself. But he said, "Father give us peace." This was not praying, he told himself.

At that point she showed him the picture of Mindy— a peculiar impulse, she decided later. She said that she used to have terrible dreams in which her child was lost and she couldn't find her. And then it happened.

He studied the picture and tears welled up in their eyes.

Tea

THE THREE OF THEM sat in the smallest room off the stage, sipping tea.

"You seem to make use of a number of psychological theories," Steiner said gently.

"*Make use of* is an interesting way of putting it. It dilutes the spontaneity involved." Jesus refilled Steiner's cup.

"Theories, religions, philosophies, feelings, thoughts, dances, laughter, ideas, meanings." Mary was going to go on but Steiner laughed and said, "OK, OK, I get the point."

"What is the point?" Jesus asked.

"The use of all there is to use," Steiner said.

"Yes," Jesus said. "Joy through fulfillment of obligation to his people."

"Integration," Mary said and then added, "Integration of everything human as applied benevolently to human beings!"

She gave each of them a huge piece of sponge cake and poured some more hot tea into their mugs from the huge teakettle she had found somewhere in the place.

Steiner left in peace but later on thought of Mary's statement about integration. He knew that these were the words of Jesus. He felt troubled.

He had the thought that she was inundated by him. How much of her was left? How could she replenish herself? He had the fleeting mind-picture of her as a bag lady.

Shadow

HE FOLLOWED PEOPLE in the street and sometimes tried to see himself in themselves and to feel what they felt.

And sometimes he knew that they were all one and that he could easily be one of them and in this way there were times he was sure he knew what they thought and there were those who knew what he thought.

He thought of what Steiner's diagnosis would be, a diagnosis of schizophrenia, paranoid type. But he didn't feel at all paranoid. He felt compassionate.

He followed a man and a child. They seemed familiar. But then he was certain this was not the man and child he had followed several weeks earlier. And the feelings that emanated from them before they disappeared were good ones.

Question

"How CAN God do these terrible things?" she asked him.

"Do them?"

"Allow them," Emily wept.

"He neither does them nor allows them."

"John has given up all ideas or beliefs he ever had. He's enraged."

"At him?"

"Yes, at him, at the world, at everyone."

"But God is not omnipotent. If God were omnipotent, Emily, there would be no free choice. People would only be his automatons. People are people because they have free choice. They have free choice because they are people. Perhaps that is why they have chosen to—or were created to—represent him."

"But they choose to do terrible things," she wept.

"They are compelled to do terrible things. Terrible things are not born of free choice. He cannot prevent terrible things from occurring. People are both sick and well—compulsive and free, monstrous and compassionate, perfectly imperfect. The cosmos is that way. God also does terrible things and wonderful things. People reflect him and his consciousness is growing."

She lost interest and felt peaceful. But a corner of herself felt empty and forever grievously wounded.

As she left he said, "Emily, nothing is forever except now."

She had no idea what he meant.

Uptown

HE CONCENTRATED on the mirror. He cleared the streets. He saw uptown streets and concentrated on one.

A man remained. He looked familiar. He tried to draw him to the place. But the man didn't move. He stood in the doorway of a store they had passed many times. His concentration didn't help at all. In fact the streets were filling up. But the man stood there. He told Mary about him. She suggested they go to see.

They took a taxi, for the first time, uptown. The streets were jammed.

When they arrived at the spot no one was there. The store itself seemed unfamiliar.

They walked the four miles back to the place. She said the streets made her feel good.

Notoriety was there.

They talked about missing children. She had written a magazine story about them three years earlier.

Then she told them about her own problem.

She couldn't sleep. Frightening dreams woke her. Sometimes she thought it was due to all the terrible things she saw and heard and wrote about. Even pills didn't work and they terrified her. She had seen several doctors and had tried psychotherapy but her sleep became even worse.

That night she slept. Jesus spent most of the night talking to his father about the missing children.

Loss

HE WAS COMFORTED by those who came to know him. But he remained distraught.

Mary was gone.

She walked out one very cold morning and did not return that night, the next day, or the next.

She was gone.

The mirror didn't work. His father remained silent. He felt powerless.

They—his friends—called hospitals, morgues, jails, etc., but she was gone. Some of them combed the streets. She was gone.

Alone

Two WEEKS had passed since Mary left.

Steiner theorized that she might have had an amnesiac attack or reverted to her bag-lady status.

He reminded himself that these were very sick people after all. Maybe she was dead.

Jesus went about in a state of mourning. Steiner realized that relative to a state of great loss, Jesus' affect was totally appropriate.

He ate, washed, walked about in a mechanical way.

Notoriety helped him with food and the dancer took over sessions on the stage.

Steiner wondered how he would do without his muse—his mother. To what extent was it a symbiotic relationship? How morbidly dependent was he on her?

Would he come apart?

Mental Status

HE did not collapse.

But his loneliness was terrible.

Why had she abandoned him? he asked a thousand

times a day. But no answer came. Was his father asleep again? The mirror reflected his face—nothing else. But the reflection of himself gave credence to his existence and comforted and calmed him.

"You are wondering," he told Steiner, "how this can happen to God's son."

Steiner said nothing.

"Remember, I've always told you that God is not omnipotent."

"How bad is it?" he asked Jesus.

"Very bad," Jesus said and tears welled up in his eyes. "I hope she is not suffering somewhere."

"But what of your suffering?"

"I'm used to it. But without her I can't work too well."

Steiner thought:

Affect appropriate.

Orientation good.

No evidence of serious disassociation.

Delusion continues.

As Steiner parted, Jesus said, "I know about loneliness and loss more than at any time before. I feel your loss as never before. Perhaps this is what he wanted me to experience."

"But you said he is not omnipotent," Steiner said.

"Not omnipotent but not without influence," Jesus answered and thought, *Is he asleep again?*

For another two thousand years?

Bus Ride

He rode the bus uptown. Forced himself to do it. Without Mary he felt terribly insecure. But he busily searched the streets and attempted to ignore the ebb and flow of his anxiety.

Then he rode the bus downtown and searched the streets on both sides as best he could.

No clue, no sign, no vibration reached him—people, loads of people, and he felt love for them all but familiarity remained dead.

At midtown, an old man with thin skin the color of old yellow wax got on the bus holding the hand of a healthy-looking, plump old lady. He thought of Mary and started to cry.

Then he had an inane association. The name Michael Tilman popped into his head. Who is Michael Tilman? he wondered. And then he suddenly knew Michael Tilman was a small boy he once knew who had been killed by a bus some twenty years earlier.

And then he saw the man. The *man*, the one he had seen with the child. *Is this why Mary left*, he thought, *to bring him here now*? He thanked his father.

He was there on the sidewalk looking at the window of the bus. He got a good look at him, medium height, nice-looking, brown hair, brown eyes, commonplace, nondescript really. But Jesus would know him anywhere.

Anywhere? But when he ran off the bus the man was gone. He looked and ran in every direction but the man was gone. He finally walked down some side streets, got himself lost, and suddenly felt himself go into a panic. "Mary, Mary," he cried but she was not there to guide him.

In panic, he ran to one of the main avenues and found his way back to the place. He had been too terrified to ask for further help from his father.

The Dream

GOD SAID, "I am awake."

Mary said, "I am alive."

God in him said, "She will return."

He woke up feeling optimistic.

He thought of going into the street but he recalled his panic the day before.

He searched the mirror but it only reflected his face and he felt dejected.

Then he heard his father's voice and it said,

"When you discovered death as a small boy you were terrified.

"But now you know. You are part of the whole. There is no getting lost, only the illusion.

"There is no life-death dichotomy, only the illusion."

He went into the streets and by chance he met a woman who had danced with them on the stage. They had coffee in a small luncheonette.

"But is there a point to it all?" she asked.

"Yes," he said.

"What?"

"Joy," he said, "and fulfillment of obligation to the species."

"Species?"

"People—doing something, anything, for people. Joy through that contribution is the point and connection to the larger self—to it all."

"If a goldfish is confined to a tank it will eat to survive. People will say it is happy just to eat. But there is nothing else it can do in the only world that exists for it." She said this with profound resignation.

"But there is much else we can do," Jesus said.

"But the mechanics of living—just getting by—puts me in a goldfish-tank world," she said.

"Like the eating goldfish, even those mechanics contribute to *your* living and you are part of the species."

"I would like the time to do more for other people but priorities of living take precedence."

"There are priorities of the mechanics of living and priorities of the heart," he replied.

"The heart?"

"The people we live for, do for, the air, the earth, the values, the commitments."

"I don't understand," she said.

"How do you feel?" he asked.

"Better," she said.

"Our talk and your feeling is time out of the tank and touches the heart."

She still didn't understand but they both felt better.

On the way back to the place, he passed a fast-food Chinese restaurant and stopped and looked through the window. He saw a boy and a girl talking to each other and from the boy's self-conscious awkwardness knew this was the boy's first date. He was so overcome with emotion he felt like crying. *The heart and its priorities*, he thought.

Memory

HE REMEMBERED waiting for her to return when he was a little boy.

He lay in bed frightened.

Then he would hear the key in the door and his fear would be gone.

She was home and he could sleep in his warm nest of a bed feeling safe and secure.

Other memories attempted to intrude but he put them down and out of his mind. These were after all from an accidental phase of his existence which had nothing to do with the *now* of his life and his father's mission for him.

Dancing helped him in this memory-clearance process and when the dancer organized the group of sixty people he danced vigorously that night.

Return

ON A FREEZING NIGHT in mid-February, forty-one days after she had left, Mary returned. It was four in the morning.

She had lost a great deal of weight. Her clothes were torn and threadbare. Her knees and knuckles bled. Her face was covered with grime. She shivered uncontrollably and said nothing.

He washed her, fed her, combed out her matted hair, changed her clothes, and put her to bed under several layers of blankets.

In the morning when she woke it was as if she had never left. She was the same as before. They did not refer to her absence then or ever again.

Interestingly, no one else did either.

But she felt replenished.

The Mirror

Two DAYS after her return he studied the mirror.

He saw his face but this did not discourage him. Indeed, it validated himself for himself and he felt very strong.

He concentrated and this time the mirror cleared.

He saw a wild-looking man talking gibberish in the street who couldn't seem to control his movements. Jesus concentrated and the man stopped talking and walked smoothly.

A teenage girl was about to walk in front of a speeding car. The girl and car stopped simultaneously.

A man about to stab another man changed his mind and threw his knife into the gutter.

A man was being encouraged by a crowd to jump from a building. The crowd dissipated and the man left the open window.

A preacher in a church said, "The road to God is not through death but through life. We all have a death sentence and a life sentence. The time between birth and death is the time between eternities. It is our time. The rest is the germinating time of the universe."

A beautiful sixteen-year-old girl with a cruelly curved spine stood straight and tall and walked gracefully and painlessly.

In a hospital bed, a cancer patient writhed in agony and then slept in peace.

A lady who was so proper that if she were any more so she would cease to exist stopped walking in the crowded street. She shouted wildly, smiled, then laughed and walked on, oblivious to the stares of people around her.

And then, with brief intervals of silence, God said:

"I am the resounding universe.

"Roma was evidence of man's will.

"Life is evidence of man's will."

In his mind he could hear Steiner say, "Roma did not die of free will but of suffering and compulsion."

"Which is also born of man," Jesus replied.

"But what of afterlife?" Steiner asked.

"Afterlife is not the concern nor within the possibility of man's comprehension."

"Can't you make me comprehend?" Steiner pleaded.

And in his mind's picture he replied,

"You want magic. *I give you humanity—his greatest magic.*"

"But I wake up from noon naps in panic—afraid of eternity," Steiner said.

"Do not be afraid. My father is the eternal, resounding universe. You will always resonate with him and will be at peace."

The Poster

IN THE MIRROR he saw the poster of the missing children.

Then he saw Emily's picture of Mindy.

Then the mirror cleared and he saw his own face.

Nothing else appeared.

But then a force from the streets to the mirror to him urged him into the street.

He obeyed and as if irresistibly guided he walked uptown to a street where he had never been before.

He recognized the man at once and the child. He simply went over to him, grasped the child's wrist, and said,

"Give me the child."

The man looked into his eyes, let go of her hand, and ran from them at a furious pace.

The Wait

THE CHILD said very little but she ate, slept, and said yes and no to their questions.

None of them knew where Emily and John lived and their phone number was unlisted. It took two days before they arrived in one of their usual sporadic night visits.

Friday Night

THEY WERE there in the audience. As soon as Jesus and Mary saw them they ran backstage and brought out the child.

John and Emily were preoccupied, talking to each other.

Mary shouted, "Emily!"

Jesus said, "John."

They looked up at the stage.

They looked at each other. Emily ran to the stage. John followed slowly and silently.

And then Emily screamed and John began to sob uncontrollably.

Mindy had changed.

She was much older.

Miracle of Compassion

By SUNDAY Mindy had told them quite a lot. The police searched for the man and suspected that a deal involving money for children had somehow gone sour in Mindy's case.

On Sunday the news was out as was the role of Jesus and much about Jesus, Mary, and the place.

A large crowd gathered at the place. There were reporters, TV cameras, and talk of heroes, heroines, and miracles. Steiner observed it all coolly.

Jesus and Mary refused to be interviewed.

A reporter asked a couple if they considered this to be a miracle.

"Miracle?" the man said. "The real miracle is how much better he, she, this place, make us feel."

There is talk of prophets. There is talk of building a church.

Steiner is not surprised.

He says out loud to no one,

"And his church is established."